TRAVELOGUE OF TERROR

A .357 revolver, spare ammunition, handcuffs, a roll of duct tape, rope, a sleeping bag, a copy of John Fowles' *The Collector*, and a fifteen-foot length of electric cord slit down the middle and fitted with a special switch—the sadistic baggage of Chris Wilder on his six-week cross-country spree of rape, torture, and murder.

Beauty queens, models, and cheerleaders were his targets, all attractive, all ambitious, and all vulnerable to this millionaire-loner's seductive but deadly charms. They all loved Chris Wilder, and he loved them too . . . loved them to death.

THE BEAUTY QUEEN KILLER

BRUCE GIBNEY

PINNACLE BOOKS
WINDSOR PUBLISHING CORP.

PINNACLE BOOKS

are published by

Windsor Publishing Corp.
475 Park Avenue South
New York, NY 10016

Second printing: March, 1990

Printed in the United States of America

Acknowledgments

The author would like to thank Julie Malear for her exhaustive research and reporting. Without her invaluable assistance, this book could not have been written.

The author would also like to thank Channing Corbin, Jack Heise, and Sam Roen; Rose Mandelsberg, editor of *Front Page Detective* magazine, for her guidance and suggestions; and the detectives who toiled diligently to track down Christopher Wilder: Ray Nazario of the Metro Dade Public Safety Department; Harvey Wasserman and George Morin, Miami Police Department; Police Officer Clifford "Mitch" Fry, Coral Gables Police Department; Detectives Tom Neighbors and Arthur Newcomb, Palm Beach County Sheriff's Office; Detective Jim Singletary, Beaumont, Texas, Police Department;

Detective John Zen, Grand Junction, Colorado, Police Department; and Sergeant Rollo Green, Torrance, California, Police Department.

The author also wishes to thank these reporters and their newspapers for providing background material and research:

Edna Buchanan, Lisa Hoffman, Dory Owens, and George Stein, *Miami Herald*; Betsy August, Tom Duboq, J. P. Faber, and Carol Marbin, *Miami News*; Michael Connelly, Rich Pollack, *Palm Beach Sun Sentinel*; Bruce Mastron, the *Tallahassee Democrat*; Joan Heller, Linda Hall, *Indian Harbour Today*; Kathy Kelly, *Daytona Beach News-Journal*; Glenn McCasland, Christopher Cook, Jenny Narkiewicz, Kevin Carmondy, *Beaumont Texas Enterprise*; Luke Clarke, James T. Bernath, Christi Foster, *Grand Junction* (Colorado) *Daily Sentinel*; Steve Chawkins, *Rocky Mountain News*; Carol Cling, Jay D. Evenson, Caryn Shetterly, Phil Pattee, *Las Vegas Review Journal*; Penny Levin, Jamie Hurly, *Las Vegas Sun*; Paul Feldman, Barry Bearak, Eric Malnic, Claire Spiegel, Jerry Belcher, John Goldman, *Los Angeles Times*; Greg Zoroya, *Torrance* (California) *Daily Breeze*; John Harrigan, Blenda Socci, Linda Renaud, Terrance Rosi, Ward Thompson, *Colebrook* (New Hampshire) *Sentinel*.

And a special note of appreciation to Lynn Dull and Teresa Hamm-Gibney, who typed the final manuscript and offered critical suggestions that proved helpful.

—Bruce Gibney
San Diego, California

THE
BEAUTY QUEEN KILLER

Chapter One

Sometime around eleven o'clock on the chilly Tuesday evening of March 20, 1984, most of the guests at the Glen Oaks Motel in rural Bainbridge, Georgia, were asleep. But in one of the neatly kept rooms, two travelers were very much awake.

One was a nineteen-year-old blonde coed from Florida State University in Tallahassee. She had been kidnapped from a shopping center near the university that afternoon and brought to the motel by a man passing himself off as a photographer.

Now, as the hour grew later, her abductor was about to indulge in yet another sadistic whim. Sliding next to her on the bed, he took a small bottle of superglue, unscrewed the cap, and tilted the nozzle toward her eye. With her hands tied and a swatch of

1

electrician's tape slapped across her mouth, she could do nothing but watch in horror as the clear, caustic glue formed a bead on the end of the nozzle, then splashed on her eyelid.

He squeezed beads of glue across the one eye so the lids were frozen together, then applied an equal amount to the other eye. Finished, he screwed the top back on the glue and then picked up a hair dryer, which he used to blow hot air onto the glue to speed the sealing time.

Once the sadistic work was done to his satisfaction, he put the hair dryer back in his travel case, stepped over the electrical wires that were taped to her toes and plugged into the wall, and sat before the TV to watch an aerobics exercise program. He became engrossed in the pretty women dressed in leotards, the camera zooming in on their breasts and flexing buttocks while they performed complicated aerobic exercises. He forgot, at least for a while, the young woman he held captive on the bed.

Bill Gaines was almost asleep in his motel room when the woman's piercing scream woke him abruptly. Throwing on a pair of pants, he charged out of his room and slammed into a man charging down the dimly lit walkway.

"Excuse me," the stranger said in a lisping accent that sounded British or Australian.

Slipping past Gaines, the man ran to a cream-colored sedan, tossed his small travel suitcase and sleeping bag into the back, and sped out of the motel parking lot, the tires kicking up rooster tails of dirt and pebbles.

Gaines continued down the walkway in search of the screams that had forced him from the comfort of his room. But they stopped as quickly as they had begun, and standing on the walkway he heard only the gusting wind in the pitch-black night and the muted roar of traffic far away on U.S. 27.

He returned to his room, puzzled by the staccato wails of pain that had been so vivid and so quickly silent, and by the man with the lisping accent who had been in such a hurry.

The night manager heard the doorbell jingle, signaling a customer, and looked up from behind the desk to see the young woman in the doorway, dressed only in a bedsheet. The bloodstains in her blonde hair, the black clumps of glue and eyelash on her cheeks, and the look of shock in her eyes told him this was no practical joke.

"Please call the police," she pleaded.

An ambulance arrived at the motel to take the young woman to Bainbridge Memorial Hospital, where she was treated for bruises and shock. Special attention was given to removing the glue, which had frozen on her lids but had not damaged the eyes.

As she was treated, Decatur County, Georgia, sheriff's detectives were busy trying to learn the identity of the man who had kidnapped and tortured the woman.

The motel clerk said a man had registered for the room at 8:15 Tuesday evening. He had paid cash for the room and signed the register with a Florida license. The clerk described him as a well-dressed man with a slight English accent. He was in his mid- or late thirties, six feet tall, and physically fit in appearance. He had a deep tan, thinning brown hair that he wore combed forward, and a thick, well-clipped beard.

Deputies searched the motel room where the girl had been held captive. They didn't find much. The man had gathered up his things before bolting out the door, and the woman had no suitcase or clothing. Only the bloodstains on the walls, a swatch of duct tape on the floor, and the unmade bed indicated the room had been occupied.

Detectives had better luck at the hospital. After receiving emergency treatment for the cuts and bruises that covered her body, the young coed talked to Chief Deputy Jim Morris.

She told the deputy that she was a nineteen-year-old freshman at Florida State University in Tallahassee. She said she had finished shopping at the Governor's Square Mall at 3:30 Tuesday afternoon and was on her way back to her car when she was approached by a man who said he was a photographer.

He said he was looking for models to pose for him and wondered if she was interested. Although she said she wasn't, he was persuasive, and said the photos would be taken at a nearby park, with no obligation.

"I'm looking for a fresh face for a fashion magazine," he said. "I think you're just the type I'm looking for."

The teenager was flattered, but wary. People had

told her she was pretty enough to be a model. But modeling was a tough racket. And careers aren't started in shopping malls by wandering photographers who happen to like your looks. Still, there was something about his manner that seemed sincere. Though persistent, he wasn't pushy and in fact seemed almost embarrassed stopping a young woman he didn't know and asking her to pose.

His appearance was also convincing. He wore a dark blue pinstriped suit with a maroon tie and an expensive-looking gold ring with a diamond inset on his left hand. He also had a Pentax camera slung casually over his shoulder, which he fiddled with as he talked.

The two went to his car, which she described as being an older model Chrysler sedan. The man showed her a number of magazines inside the vehicle and a portfolio of magazine covers and fashion layouts he claimed were his work. He said he was not interested in nude modeling and that he didn't do nudes. He said high-fashion magazines were interested only in faces and figures that displayed clothing well. He said the shooting would take less than an hour and that he would pay her $25.

The coed thanked him for the offer but said she couldn't do it and started to leave. She said the man spun her around by the shoulder and drove a fist into her stomach that made her double over. He hit her in the face and pushed her into the car. They drove to a wooded area behind the shopping mall, where he slapped a piece of duct tape across her mouth and tied her hands. They drove to a rest area near Bradfordville, north of Tallahassee, where she was hog-tied with rope and pushed into the trunk of the car.

The woman said she didn't know how long she remained in the trunk, but it seemed like hours. When they stopped and she was pulled out, it was pitch dark. The kidnapper pulled a sleeping bag over her, zipped it up, and put her into the back seat. When they reached the motel, he slung her over his shoulder like a meat carcass and carried her into the room.

She said she didn't know where she was or even what state she was in. Her abductor told her if she attempted to escape or summon help, he would kill her. With her hands tied and the tape across her mouth, she was at his mercy.

For the rest of the evening, she was subjected to sexual humiliation and torture. It began when he lay down next to her nude body and masturbated while watching the television. Later he forced her to perform oral sex and raped her twice.

The nightmare continued as he removed a fifteen-foot electrical cord from his suitcase, attached the copper wire ends to her legs, and administered electrical shocks by a switch he controlled manually.

She said he then attempted to glue her eyes shut with the bottle of superglue he had brought along for the occasion. The glue clung to her eyelashes, but she managed to peek through the cemented lashes.

With her feet still wired to the electrical cord, her abductor ordered her to mimic the aerobic show he was watching on TV. She danced while he remained frozen in front of the television.

She said later that as he watched the TV, she edged over to the bathroom door and pulled the electrical wire out of the wall and tried to escape. He scrambled to his feet and they struggled. She said he grabbed the hair dryer and hit her over the head, splitting her scalp. She fought back, getting an eye gouged in the process. With blood streaming down her face, she ran into the bathroom, locked the door, and began screaming and pounding on the walls.

The man then panicked, grabbed up as many things as he could, including his suitcase and all of her clothing, and fled out the door. The woman waited about thirty minutes before opening the bathroom door. She wrapped a sheet around herself and went to the manager for help.

The sheriff's office issued an all-points bulletin on the assailant, with a detailed description of the suspect and the car in which he fled the motel. The woman said she thought she saw an official document in the front seat that looked like an Australian passport.

The bulletin was telexed to law-enforcement agencies in Georgia, Mississippi, Alabama, and Florida, and to the FBI, where it received close attention.

The Bureau had been investigating the disappearances of two aspiring models in South Florida, both of whom bore a striking resemblance to the nineteen-year-old Florida State freshman kidnapped from Tallahassee on Tuesday afternoon.

There was also another common thread that linked

the three Florida women: all had been last seen with a handsome, well-dressed man in his late thirties who spoke with an accent and fancied himself a photographer.

Chapter Two

"Sure I know Chris Wilder," said the Texaco gas station attendant. "He comes in here to buy gas all the time. I know him pretty well. I guess I would call him a friend. He's got to be the nicest person I know."

It seemed no one in the torpid South Florida community of Boynton Beach had anything bad to say about Christopher Bernard Wilder. In fact, many openly wished to trade places with him.

A jaunty thirty-eight-year-old millionaire who still spoke with the slight accent of his native Australia, Wilder was living a bachelor's fantasy life in this little resort community south of Palm Beach. He owned a plush home, complete with Jacuzzi and an indoor-outdoor pool, raced sports cars at the Miami

Grand Prix and Sebring, and never hurt for female companionship.

A photographer friend named Ted Marton described him as "a rich playboy who loved women, racing, and the jet set. He liked to throw money around. He loved to be around two or three women at a time, and you're talking about elegant ladies, long legs, younger than he."

Wilder was the most visible advocate of the good life on Mission Hill Road, a street of manicured lawns and well-tended homes owned by upper-income families. His posh bachelor pad was set back off the road and was secluded by fencing and thick shrubbery. Still, it was hard not to notice the steady stream of girls who came and went to the house—some of them street-type girls, some of them looking like models, a few of them walking in with suitcases and staying for a week or two. The windows were always shaded, but on a still night, with a balmy breeze blowing off the ocean, neighbors could hear the titter of female laughter and the sound of people splashing in the pool.

It was perhaps a measure of the Australian's charismatic personality that his neighbors liked Wilder despite these intrusions on their privacy.

"He had his parties, but they weren't so bad," said a suburban matron who lived across the street. "If things got too noisy, he would come by the next morning and apologize. He had his life and we had ours, but he always said hello when we saw him and asked how we were doing. And unlike a lot of people these days, I think he actually meant it."

Two persons taken with the Australian's charm were William and Delores Kenyon of Pompano Beach. They met him socially a few times and liked him. But that brief friendship ended the second week in March 1984, when their daughter Beth disappeared.

Her disappearance triggered a week-long nightmare that on a balmy evening took Bill Kenyon and his son to the playboy pad on Mission Hill Road armed with a .38 and determined to get some answers.

Twenty-three-year-old Beth Kenyon was a stunningly beautiful woman, physically perfect, with alluring, almond-shaped eyes, luxuriant brown hair that fell in curls far below her slender shoulders, and a wide, toothy grin worthy of a television ad.

Her eye-turning looks had earned her the title of 1982 Orange Bowl Princess and made her a finalist in the Miss Florida contest. Fresh from these triumphs, Beth had given thought to a full-time career as a fashion model. She had done local modeling and had contacts in New York, but she had doubts, wondering if that was really what she wanted to do. In 1983 she decided to put her modeling career on hold, at least for a while, and in the fall took a teaching job at Coral Gables High School south of Miami.

Her first year was very difficult. She taught classes for emotionally disturbed youngsters. After school she was a cheerleading coach and attended as many as three basketball games a week.

For the daughter of the closely knit, wealthy Pompano Beach family, the experience was eye-opening. There were emotional crises and fights between students almost daily in the sprawling high school, with teachers often caught in the middle. She had already saved one suicidal student who had slit her wrists, and spent one night at the Jackson Memorial Hospital Rape Center comforting a schoolgirl who had been assaulted.

Beth had confided to other teachers that she was disappointed in teaching. They tried to cheer her up, but there wasn't much they could do. Teaching at Coral Gables High wasn't an easy job, more Blackboard Jungle than Our Mister Chips, and teaching emotionally deprived students was one of the hardest assignments. Her friends urged her to stay, but Beth didn't know. She said she would last the school year and then play it by ear.

Away from the high school, Beth lived with a roommate in a singles apartment complex on Coral Gables's Ives Dairy Road but made weekly trips to Pompano Beach to be with her parents. When she arrived at the family's plush home on Sunday, March 4, her father noticed bruises on his daughter's arms and legs.

"What happened?" he asked.

Schoolyard fight, Beth had replied matter-of-factly. She got caught in the middle trying to separate two students.

At nine P.M. Beth kissed her father good night, got behind the wheel of her sporty Chrysler convertible, and headed back in the darkness for Coral Gables.

After she left, the family watched the eleven o'clock news on TV. A picture of a beautiful girl flashed on the screen. She had long dark hair that fell past her shoulders, large dark eyes, and a pretty, innocent smile. "That looks like Beth," said her brother, Bill Junior. And it did too. The photo was of a twenty-year-old Homestead woman named Rosario Gonzalez, who had been missing since February 26. The name, for the moment, meant nothing to the Kenyons.

Beth returned to her apartment a few minutes after ten o'clock, slipped into a nightgown, and thumbed through a woman's magazine before going to bed. The following morning she rose early to get ready for classes. The day went without incident for a change, and at three o'clock her school day was through. She headed for the faculty parking lot to get her car. One of the last persons she talked to was Clifford "Mitch" Fry, a Coral Gables police officer assigned to the high school. The two had become friends after Beth started teaching, and she often told him "horror stories" detailing the grim realities of teaching high school in the 1980s.

"Today was quiet for a change," Beth laughed. "Must be spring-break fever."

Mitch smiled. Even at prosperous high schools like Coral Gables, the days were few and far between when teachers could teach and not worry about drug deals going down in the bathrooms or students being assaulted in the parking lots.

The two chatted for a few moments before Beth got into her car and drove home.

The following Tuesday afternoon Mitch was called to the office of an assistant principal of the high school. Had he seen Beth today? the assistant principal asked. She hadn't shown up for her morning classes.

No, he hadn't seen her, he said. Not since Monday afternoon.

Mitch called Beth's apartment and got her roommate. She was also worried. Beth hadn't been home Monday night. She hadn't called or communicated in any way. That was unlike her, out of character.

Beth's parents were also worried. Their daughter had said nothing about a trip or seeing anyone when she left their home Sunday. And they knew her well enough to know she would not walk away from her job, no matter how bad it got. She had expressed reservations about teaching, but Beth was no quitter. She would have gone to her classes on Tuesday—unless something had happened to her. That evening the Kenyons telephoned all the friends listed in Beth's address books. They also checked with local law enforcement agencies and the area hospitals. No one had seen her.

Out of places to look, Bill Kenyon made out a missing-persons report on Beth. The officer at the Metro Dade Public Safety Department station appeared almost bored as he pushed the single-page form across the counter. After the Kenyons left, the report was put in a file with the others made out in the past few days, where it was promptly forgotten.

While the Kenyons searched for Beth, Mitch Fry had begun his own investigation. The Coral Gables cop went to her apartment on Ives Dairy Road and found nothing that indicated she had left town unexpectedly. Her luggage was still there, her clothes were in the closet, and her makeup and toothbrush were still in the bathroom. Mitch took her personal directory and called every name listed in it. One of the last numbers called was Christopher Wilder's. Fry identified himself and left a message on Wilder's answering machine. Wilder never bothered to call back.

Chapter Three

Christopher Bernard Wilder was born March 13, 1945, the oldest of four sons of a U.S. Navy career man and his Australian wife, who met in Sydney during World War II.

The Wilders moved to the United States after the war, the first of several trips between their native homelands, before they decided to live permanently in Australia. In the early 1960s they settled in New South Wales, where the retired naval officer began a lucrative career in the booming construction business.

Three times the Wilders almost lost their oldest son. Shortly after birth, Christopher was given the last rites because he was not expected to live. As a toddler he was found floating facedown in the family swimming pool and was revived at the last moment.

At age three he lapsed into a coma in his parents' car while on a cross-country trip, and his breathing became labored. Then, as it appeared he might die, Christopher regained consciousness.

When he grew older, Wilder rarely talked about his three early brushes with death. Instead, he preferred to tell his friends about the good swimming and surfing found near his New South Wales home and the pretty young girls who strolled the beaches in swimsuits much smaller than the ones found in the United States.

Wilder accompanied his family when they returned to Australia for good in the early 1960s. But after graduating from high school, he decided he liked America better, and moved to Florida in 1969.

An early marriage fizzled after just eight days and he sought a beach bum existence in the Gold Coast beach towns between Palm Beach and Miami, surfing and swimming as much as he could and using carpenter skills learned in high school to pick up jobs in the construction business.

By the mid-1970s he had been in and out of several businesses, including a topless bar in Miami, and had moved up several notches on the economic scale. He was living in swank $600-a-month apartments and driving expensive sports cars, which he sold or traded in every year.

In 1979 the cocky, self-assured Australian hocked his construction tools for $2,500 and with another gutsy, ambitious entrepreneur named L. K. Kimbrell, began electrical contracting and construction businesses. The firms were Sawtel Electric and Sawtel Construction, named after a fashionable beach resort in Australia where Wilder had spent many a happy weekend in his youth.

The two contractors landed fat contracts with developers that were building a massive condominium village near Boynton Beach. Business boomed and within three years Wilder's $2,500 investment had boomed into a business that employed seventy people.

Wilder used his share of the profits to wheel and deal his way to a personal fortune approaching $2 million. Most went into real estate: properties in Boynton Beach and Fort Lauderdale, undeveloped lots in suburban Wellington, two homes in the suburbs south of Palm Beach, and the building on Northeast Third Avenue that housed the Sawtel companies. He also was a corporate officer in the Wild Palm Kennels, Inc., in Fort Lauderdale.

Something of an overnight success, Wilder adopted a life-style that fit a young bachelor who didn't mind indulging his pleasures. He remodeled the house he bought on Mission Hill Road with parquet floors, installed a Jacuzzi off the bedroom, and built an indoor-outdoor pool that overlooked the canal in back and featured a map of his native Australia tiled on the bottom.

He then spent most of his afternoons and evenings filling his aquatic installations with young women he met at singles bars or saw strolling on the beach. If splashing in the pool to music piped in through the $5,000 sound system didn't do the trick, he could always take his dates on a late night ride in the speedboat that hung on twin derricks and swung out over the canal that ran through the backyard. Or they could hop into the charcoal-gray Cadillac or customized Porsche Carrera and ride to a singles hangout like the Banana Boat or Poppa Joe's, or maybe cruise down to the jai alai court in Miami or the racetrack in Hialeah.

In 1982 Wilder took up sports car racing. He entered amateur races in Miami and Daytona and was listed with International Motor Sports of America, the racing association based in Bridgeport, Connecticut.

Wilder was never much more than a middle-of-the-pack driver. He raced five times as an amateur in 1982, and competed in three races as a professional. He never finished better than halfway back in the pack and his winnings were a measly $750. But Wilder loved the fast cars and the camaraderie found on the racing circuit almost as much as the steady stream of girls that found their way to his home.

It was the good life, and Wilder couldn't get enough of it. He spent more time at the beach or racing his cars than he did at the office, much to the dismay of his partner, L. K. Kimbrell.

"I think you can see where his interests lay," Kimbrell said, showing a reporter Wilder's office. On the walls were framed photos of race cars and Wilder's racing buddies, while in the closet was a single item: Wilder's racing suit.

His partner might grumble, but Wilder reasoned he had worked hard to make the company a success, and he was tired of the rat race.

"This is a new change in myself," he admitted.

"I'm going to start doing some getting out and away, specifically from work."

And who could argue? A decade earlier he had arrived in his adopted country with little more than a frayed suitcase and a desire to surf.

"I only went into business after I learned Florida didn't have surf," he liked to joke. If so, the joke wasn't on him. He had his own business, almost $2 million in assets, and a life-style the readers of *Playboy* magazine yearned for.

"You could look at Chris and say, 'Wow, that's what I would like to be doing!' " a racing pal said of his friend. "Everybody liked him, and he didn't have a care in the world. He was one hundred percent happy. What more could you ask for?"

Chapter Four

By Thursday, March 8, Bill Kenyon reached the conclusion that the Metro Dade police were not going to help him find his daughter. The single-page report he had filled out on Tuesday was still stuck in missing persons, where it remained, uninvestigated.

If his daughter was going to be found, Kenyon would have to take the initiative. That afternoon he called Kenneth Whittaker Investigative Consultants, a prestigious private eye firm located in North Miami.

The chief investigator was Kenneth Whittaker Junior, a twenty-eight-year-old law school graduate, and son of Kenneth Whittaker Senior, an attorney and the former special agent in charge of the FBI office in Miami. The boyish, sandy-haired gumshoe listened patiently as Kenyon detailed his unhappiness with

Metro Dade before agreeing to search for the missing twenty-three-year-old beauty queen at his normal rate of $1,000 a day. Kenyon wrote out a check and Whittaker went to work that evening.

Looking through letters and personal mementos that were in the missing girl's room, and questioning her friends, the private investigator learned Beth had gone on a dinner date with a West German business-man who had flown in to see a mutual friend in Miami. The dinner had been pleasant, if a bit difficult—the West German didn't speak English—and Beth expressed no interest in seeing him again when she came home that night.

Whittaker also talked to one of Beth's old boy-friends, a lawyer with the state attorney's office in Tampa. The two had broken up but recently were seeing each other again. The Tampa attorney had said he could get her a $1,500 assignment modeling skiwear in Colorado Springs. Beth had sounded ex-cited by the offer when she came home and told her roommate. She was also looking forward to seeing her old flame.

"He doesn't know it, but I just might marry that man," she told her roommate.

But Beth didn't go to Colorado Springs, and the detective learned the job went to someone else.

Still another name on the private eye's checklist was that of an old boyfriend named Christopher Wilder. The two had met in 1982 when Beth entered the Miss Florida contest. After the judging, Wilder had come backstage, introduced himself as a professional photographer, and asked her out on a date.

Beth normally said no to such offers. "She would never go out with somebody unless he was a friend of someone she knew," her mother said. "I used to call her Mother Hubbard."

But this time she said yes. They dined on crepes at a Pompano Beach restaurant near the Kenyon home. Wilder was charming and his manners impeccable. He drove her back to her apartment and said he wanted to see her again. Beth said she would like that.

"Photographers are always making passes or asking me to model nude," Beth told her mother. "Chris is different; he's the perfect gentleman."

Wilder regaled her with stories of surfing and adventure in his native Australia. He called it a paradise and said he wanted to take her back there and make her a princess. Nothing was too good for her. He offered to pay her way through an auto-racing school. When she forgot her sunglasses on the way to an automobile race he was entered in, he stopped at Lord & Taylor's and chose a $40 pair.

After the first few dates, Chris proposed to her.

"She was kind of laughing about it, a little amazed," her mother recalled. "She said, 'Mom, I've never even kissed the guy and he asked me to marry him.' "

Beth turned him down; she wasn't ready for marriage, and with a seventeen-year gap in their ages Chris was just too old—but they remained good friends.

Beth's parents liked Chris. "He had a way of

listening to problems; he was real sincere,'' her father said. ''I knew he loved her deeply. They had a way of communicating with each other.''

Whittaker's interest was aroused when he learned Beth had mentioned Wilder the day before she vanished. She had returned a week earlier from New York from a visit with the family of ABC sports announcer Jim McKay, whose son she dated. She said she'd had a wonderful time, but was a little sad too.

''Chris had me set up with a modeling job as Miss Budweiser at the Grand Prix in Miami,'' she told her parents. ''It would have paid four thousand dollars.''

She had sounded wistful at missing the opportunity.

Whittaker called Wilder and asked if he had seen Beth. Wilder replied no, he had been out of town for a couple of days and hadn't seen Beth for over a month. Why, had something happened to her?

Wilder seemed the last person in the world to be suspected of kidnapping the young woman. Beth had turned down his marriage proposal, but that had been two years prior, and there was no reason to believe Chris held hard feelings. Chris still cared for Beth, but they were friends, not lovers. And Chris had all those other women to occupy his time.

Beth's parents liked Chris; there was no reason to suspect he knew anything about Beth's disappearance. Their opinion, however, quickly changed.

Ron Stone, an insurance man and president of the University of Miami, had dated Beth, and when he learned she had disappeared, he tried to help. He stopped by gas stations where Beth normally bought gas and showed her picture to the attendants.

At the Shell station on Bird and Douglas roads in Coral Gables, an attendant named Ricky remembered Beth stopping two days before—Monday afternoon, March 5.

She offered to pay with a credit card, he recalled, but a man in a charcoal-gray Cadillac pulled up behind her and paid for her gas with a $20 bill.

"The two seemed to know each other," Ricky said. "I started to wipe the windshield and Beth said, 'Forget it, we have to get to the airport.' "

Beth then turned to the man and asked how she looked.

"Just fine," the man replied.

"Who's going to take the picture?" Beth asked.

"I am," he replied. "Come on, let's go."

Ricky described the man as in his mid- or late thirties, about six feet tall, trim and tan, with light brown hair that was balding on top, and a beard.

"Beth said she was going to the airport," the attendant said. "It sounded like she had to catch a plane or something. She didn't seem nervous or uptight, and neither did the guy. They were real friendly."

Whittaker went to the Kenyon home in Pompano Beach, and with the father's permission removed from Beth's photo album all the snapshots of the men she had dated. He returned to the gas station the following morning and showed the pictures one at a time to the attendant.

Halfway through the stack of cards, the attendant pointed to one showing Beth and a man standing at the racetrack ticket window. "That's him," the attendant said. "That's the one that was driving the Caddie."

The photo was of Christopher Wilder.

Ken Whittaker Senior called Wilder at his home, identified himself as an attorney representing the Kenyons, and asked if he knew Beth.

"Sure I do," replied Wilder.

"Have you seen her lately?" Whittaker asked.

"No," Wilder replied. "I haven't seen Beth for at least one month."

Whittaker sensed Wilder was nervous and was about to hang up. "Not so fast, Chris," the attorney said. "We have a guy down here who saw you at a gas station with Beth on Monday."

"That's impossible," Wilder shouted into the receiver. "I haven't seen Beth in a long time."

"Okay," Whittaker said. "But will you do me a favor and call the Kenyons and assure them you know nothing about this?"

"Absolutely," Wilder said. "I'll call them after I hang up. A terrible mistake's been made."

That evening Mrs. Kenyon got a call. It was Wilder. "I like you, I like Beth," he said. "What's going on? Why is this man Whittaker calling me?"

She said everyone associated with Beth was being investigated.

"But I don't know anything about her disappearance," he said. "Now this private eye says he found a guy who saw me with Beth the day she dropped out of sight. And that's impossible. The witness is mistaken.''

Bill Kenyon didn't think so. He had spent one of the most frustrating weeks of his life trying to get a police department—any police department—interested in finding his daughter. After Wilder was identified by the gas station attendant he knew in his heart who had taken his daughter.

He called Metro Dade, but missing persons was closed on the weekends and he was told to call Monday. He tried other agencies, but they were closed, or said missing persons wasn't their responsibility.

Kenyon called the Boynton Beach police. They said it was out of their jurisdiction—try the Miami police. In desperation he telephoned the sheriff of Niagara County, New York, the Kenyons' home when not in Florida. "Nobody wants to help us," Bill Kenyon said. "They all give us the brush-off."

The New York lawmen said the sheriff of Palm Beach County was a personal friend and to drop his name. Kenyon called Palm Beach. The sheriff was out and a gravel-voiced lieutenant answered. "I'm sorry," the lieutenant said, "but it's out of our jurisdiction."

Kenyon hung up the phone with tears in his eyes. No one cared. No one wanted to help him find his daughter.

That Saturday evening Kenyon and his son, Bill Junior, drove up to Boynton Beach and staked out Wilder's home. At one point the younger Kenyon slipped through the bushes to take down the tag number on a trailer in the driveway.

Bill Kenyon had taken a .38 revolver along on the trip. His son suggested they take Wilder at gunpoint, stick the barrel in his gut, and force him to talk. Kenyon nixed the idea. They were going to play this one by the book; they would not break the law.

They returned home and telephoned Mitch Fry, Beth's friend with the Coral Gables Police Department and the only police officer to show an interest in the case. Kenyon asked if he should have the investigator watch the house.

Fry said by all means. "You have the money, you have a private detective. He has the manpower; watch the house."

The next morning, Sunday, March 11, investigators Ken Whittaker and Mike Fornelo drove up to Boynton Beach to question the thirty-nine-year-old contractor. They didn't find him at his home, where the Sunday paper sat on the doorstop and Wilder's three English setters barked inside. Nor did they spot him at DJ's diner, where he had his steak-and-eggs breakfasts. Or at the Banana Boat or Poppa Joe's. No one had seen him or knew where he was.

On the way back to Miami, the detectives stopped off at the Boynton Beach Police Department and asked a detective in major-crimes detail if he knew anything about Christopher Wilder.

The detective's jaw dropped a foot. "We have a file on him two inches thick," the detective said.

The weighty file showed a dark side to Wilder's personality, one he had struggled to conceal for much of his adult life, and which he had been able to keep secret from even his closest friends.

Chapter Five

In 1977 a broken and sobbing Christopher Wilder confessed to psychologist Dr. D. G. Boozer that he had sexually molested a sixteen-year-old girl after luring her into his car.

"I was feeling down in the dumps," Wilder admitted. "I saw her and something came over me. I knew it was wrong, but I did it anyway."

Wilder was building a winding staircase in a Boca Raton home when he spotted the family's sixteen-year-old daughter walk out the door. She was pretty, about five feet, six inches tall, with a shapely figure and long light brown hair that fell past her shoulders. Just the type of girl Wilder was obsessed with.

He struck up a conversation and asked her what she wanted to do after high school. Be a secretary, she replied. That was wonderful, he said, he could use a secretary. He wanted to know if she would be interested in an interview for a job right then. She said she would, and got into his pickup truck.

About a mile away from home, the girl grew worried and asked to be taken home. Wilder pulled off the road near a roadway stop and said he couldn't do that. When she attempted to bolt, he grabbed her by the arm and slapped her hard across the face.

"You are goddamn going to do what I want," Wilder raged, ripping at her clothes.

To fend him off the girl said she had a venereal disease, hoping her lie would save her life. She survived to press charges, but not before she was forced to have oral sex with him.

On the way back to Boca Raton, a repentant Wilder said he knew what he had done was wrong and asked if she wanted to go home or to the police. Home, she requested. Her parents called the police.

The electrical contractor was arrested and charged with the sexual assault upon the Boca Raton teenager. When examined in a pretrial evaluation, Dr. Boozer deemed the successful contractor a "psychotic," who, when left to his own resources and under stress, disintegrated.

"He is not safe except in a structured environment and should be in a resident program geared to his needs," Boozer concluded.

The second examiner, a psychiatrist, did not go so far, finding Wilder troubled but not psychotic, but also concurring that Wilder should receive structured and supervised treatment for his illness.

Amenable to treatment, Wilder told his attorney, Nelson Bailey, "I will plead guilty and get therapy, anything they want. I need help. But I don't want to go to jail, I am terrified of jail."

It was a good deal, as plea bargains go. Wilder did not have a police record, and the guilty plea meant the state had some control over him. He would receive the supervised treatment suggested by the psychologist and psychiatrist and might possibly be cured. If he wasn't, and he was convicted of a second sexual offense, Wilder would go to prison.

But a Palm Beach County judge rejected the offer, ordering Wilder to stand trial.

"The judge believes that if you commit a sex offense, you go to prison," Bailey explained to his client. "The judge took the attitude the public wants him to take."

The hard-line stand backfired when a Palm Beach jury took just fifty-five minutes to find Wilder not guilty.

The jubilant contractor pumped his attorney's hand and walked out of the courthouse a free man. He still could have sought psychiatric help, but without the threat of imprisonment hanging over his head, he didn't bother.

Three years later two vacationing teenage girls from Tennessee were approached in a West Palm Beach shopping center by a photographer, who gave his name as "David Pierce." He told them he was shooting pictures for a pizza ad and needed models. The girls agreed to model. It sounded like a come-on, but they were curious and the photographer seemed sincere.

He told them he wanted them to look sexy and took them to stores, where they tried on shorts and spike heels. One of the girls went back to the home where she was staying while the other decided to stay with the photographer, who said he would make her famous.

They went to a restaurant where he ordered her a slice of pizza.

"Chew it slowly," he instructed. "I want to see what it looks like."

When the teenager complained of feeling drowsy, he told her to look deeply into his eyes. "My eyes are the camera," he said.

He took her to his pickup truck parked in the mall lot, where he had her lay down on the front seat. He slipped his hands inside her blouse and began massaging her breasts. When the girl asked if that was necessary, he said yes, it was. "You want to be a Barbizon model, don't you?"

The girl removed her blouse, and he crawled into the cab. When she resisted he raped her.

The girl got the license-plate number of the pickup and gave it to the police. The next day Christopher Wilder was picked up and brought to the West Palm Beach sheriff's station.

"I don't know what happened," Wilder told Detective Arthur Newcomb. "I have some sexual problems and have been seeing a psychiatrist. My job is my whole life. On the weekdays I am okay, then on the weekends something happens."

Wilder was charged with the rape, but instead of a trial, he was allowed to plead guilty to a lesser charge of attempted sexual battery. Circuit Judge John Wessel placed him on five years probation, during which he was required to undergo psychological counseling with a sex therapist.

Wilder's attorney, Nelson Bailey, was a bit surprised that the prosecutor agreed to deal. "The state was sitting there with the copies of the psychiatric evaluation that recommended hospitalization. This was a second offense. There was a very legitimate reason to prosecute."

Prosecutor Donald Bicknel said he had no choice. "Had this case gone to trial, without a doubt Wilder would have been found not guilty," Bicknel said. "There were no eyewitnesses and the physical evidence was inconclusive. The girl said she felt drugged after eating the pizza, but the lab technicians could find no trace of drugs. It was a one-on-one situation, in which juries consistently find the person not guilty. So we went with what we had. I thought we were fortunate to get what we did."

Wilder cooperated fully with the terms of his probation, made regular visits to his probation officer, and saw a sex therapist. His probation officer wrote in his report that Wilder was making progress and seemed sincere in his efforts to rehabilitate himself.

One of the conditions of Wilder's parole was that he not use false identities or misrepresent himself. Unknown to the parole officer, Wilder called up the Tide Talent modeling agency in Palm Beach and offered his services as a photographer. The owner,

Tom Davis, declined the offer, saying the agency used only established photographers.

Wilder soon started showing up at the office with a camera slung over one shoulder. He also started collecting business cards from professional photographers, which he passed out to the pretty young women he stopped in the shopping malls.

In December 1982 he made a trip to Australia to see his family. On December 22, two fifteen-year-old girls were kidnapped from a beach in New South Wales and taken to a park, where they were stripped and forced to take part in pornographic picture taking. The girls were then bound, forced into a car, and driven to a motel for more posing.

Their abductor, the girls said, had introduced himself as a photographer and handed them business cards from the Tide Talent Agency in Palm Beach, Florida.

Sydney police traced the car used in the assault to Christopher Wilder. Arrested the following day, he was charged with kidnapping and indecent assault. His passport was lifted, and he was ordered to appear for trial on May 7.

Wilder, however, claimed he could not stay in Australia until his trial and had to return to Miami or risk losing hundreds of thousands of dollars in business contracts. His passport was returned and he was allowed to go, but only after his parents agreed to put up $350,000 bail.

His scrapes with the law hardly put a dent in his flamboyant life-style back in the U.S. He still made the rounds of his favorite nightclubs, and women continued to stream into his Mission Hill Road home.

He also kept his appointments with his probation officer and his twice-a-month sessions with the sex therapist. To them, Wilder was making steady improvement. But beneath the calm, confident exterior churned a personality dangerously out of control.

One of his closest friends was a secretary who worked for a company Sawtel Electric did business for. They had dated briefly, then remained friends, seeing each other to have lunch or just to talk. After the 1980 arrest for assaulting the Tennessee teenager, Wilder said he started having blackouts.

"Chris would disappear for two or three days at a time," the woman said later. "He would come back really shaken. I asked him where he had gone and what he had done, and he said he didn't know. He told me that when he had these blackouts it was as if someone had just stolen those days out of his life."

The blackouts diminished when he started the sex therapy sessions, but after returning from Australia, Wilder complained the blackouts were coming back and now were bothering him all the time.

Chapter Six

The two detectives drove back to Miami that evening, convinced they had found the person responsible for Beth Kenyon's disappearance. They didn't know where she was, or even if she was still alive, but they felt the answers would be found back in Boynton Beach.

The following morning William Kenyon and his son went to the Boynton Beach police station, where they learned for the first time the extent of Christopher Wilder's secret life. Both men were outraged and demanded Wilder's arrest. Lieutenant John Hollihan said that wasn't possible because a crime had not been committed in Boynton Beach. Beth's brother became so enraged that it seemed the only one who might go to jail would be him.

The Kenyons left the police station frustrated

that they could not get police interested in arresting Wilder.

The private investigators, however, had better luck. Ken Whittaker Junior and Bill Murphy, a twenty-eight-year-old ex-police officer, parked across from the Sawtel Construction office and waited. At two that afternoon a slate-gray Cadillac pulled into the parking lot and Christopher Wilder, dressed in dark slacks and a pink polo shirt, stepped out.

The two detectives identified themselves before he reached the door, and asked if they could talk in his office.

Wilder shrugged and said, "Why not?"

Inside the paneled office with the framed photos of racing cars on the walls, Wilder repeated that he had not seen Beth for almost a month and had not been at the gas station with her the day she disappeared.

"I've been mistaken for someone else," he said.

He punched a button on the intercom and a secretary walked in and sat next to him across the table from the detectives. She said Wilder had been spending mornings in Boca Raton on a project and his afternoons in the office.

The detectives told the secretary that they were investigating the disappearance of Beth Kenyon.

"Oh, yeah," she replied. "The girl whose car was found at the airport."

The private eyes exchanged looks; they had said nothing about finding Beth's car.

Turning to Wilder the secretary said, "That's what you told me, isn't it?"

"Oh, yes," Wilder said. "Mrs. Kenyon told me that."

The detectives said they still wanted Wilder to appear in a lineup later in the week.

"Sure, I have no complaints," Wilder said. "I wasn't anywhere near Miami on Monday, but if it will help you any way, I'll certainly be glad to."

After leaving the office, Whittaker contacted the Kenyon home and asked Mrs. Wilder if she had told Wilder about finding Beth's car.

"No, I didn't," she replied, "I never brought it up."

The detectives returned to Miami, convinced that Wilder was behind the kidnapping of Beth Kenyon despite the assurances that he had been in the office on the afternoon he was supposedly spotted at the Miami gas station.

The Kenyons were also satisfied that Wilder was behind their daughter's disappearance. They placed calls to Metro Dade police and the FBI to explain what they had uncovered, in hopes the agencies might start investigations. But the FBI said they couldn't do anything, and Metro Dade still saw no reason to turn the missing persons report over to detective detail, which was already swamped by unsolved cases.

While the Kenyon case went uninvestigated, a similar missing persons case was receiving the full treatment by the Miami Police Department homicide investigators.

"Every now and then we get a case that, after

talking to the parents and friends, we don't think is a runaway," said Detective Harvey Wasserman. "And we jumped on this one right away."

Although twenty-year-old Rosario Gonzalez had never met Beth Kenyon, they shared several things in common: both had entered the Miss Florida contest, both wanted to pursue modeling careers, and both were attracted to race-car driving. They also, police learned, knew Chris Wilder.

Early Sunday morning Rosario left her comfortable middle-class home in Homestead, south of Miami, for the Miami Grand Prix track, where she had a job distributing aspirin samples. The job lasted two days and Rosario had been guaranteed $400. Police learned she arrived at the track at 8:30 A.M. and picked up her sample tray containing the aspirin at the drug company's tent.

Dressed in skimpy red shorts and a T-shirt with the company logo written across the front, she worked the crowd, perhaps thinking of her June wedding. The night before, she'd discussed it long distance with her fiancé until almost two in the morning, excited at the many plans they were making. "I love you so much it hurts," she told him over the phone.

For four or five hours, she worked near the corner of Flagler Street on the east side of Biscayne Boulevard. She returned to the company tent between noon and one P.M. and dropped off her sample tray. She picked up her purse, and without picking up her $400 check for the two days' work, she headed toward the parking lot. One other young woman, also chosen to distribute aspirin samples, saw her go but thought Rosario was taking a lunch break.

The young woman was supposed to return to her home in Homestead, Florida, between six and seven o'clock that evening. She didn't, and by nine her parents began calling the police and the Florida Highway Patrol for accident reports. Next they called the hospitals. In the past Rosario had always called if she was going to be late. They were sure something had happened.

"By three A.M.," her mother said, "we were so hysterical, screaming and crying, we couldn't control our emotions long enough to say a prayer."

The City of Miami Police Department homicide detail was on the case early the following day. Detectives George Morin and Harvey Wasserman were assigned to the case. They began by interviewing the family, the aspirin company and promoters, and friends of the family. A day later police located a man who had been taking pictures of the pretty woman. He turned out to be a friend of the family. He was given a polygraph test and passed.

On Wednesday, February 29, the first news story of Rosario's disappearance appeared in the *Miami Herald*. Another model and her mother read the story and told police they remembered Rosario walking away with a man in his mid- or late thirties. They described him to a police artist, and the drawing was distributed to the media with an appeal for help.

A tipster told the detectives he thought he saw the missing woman cavorting with a man aboard a yacht in the Miami River. "The girl was real pretty and had on these skimpy shorts," he said. The police found the yacht and questioned the woman. She was not Rosario.

Two days and a dozen tips later, a Miami fire fighter gave detectives the last known photos of Rosario. He had snapped them at the race the day she vanished. They showed her seated on a stone step, her hands clasped in front of her legs, a diamond engagement ring on one finger. Her almond-shaped eyes crinkled at the corners as her full mouth broke into a pretty smile. It was the last picture Rosario's parents would have of their daughter; she looked wonderfully happy.

"This girl was perfect," said her twenty-one-year-old fiancé, William Londos. "She was so innocent and sweet. The first time I saw her I said, this is the kind of girl you marry."

Looking at Rosario's picture, the detectives felt the same way. From descriptions given by dozens of witnesses, they determined the girl had not left home on a whim, or taken off with another man, or any of the dozens of other reasons people decide to walk away, leaving friends and family wondering what happened.

"We figured she had been kidnapped," Detective Wasserman told a reporter weeks after her disappearance. "We don't know if she is alive."

Leads continued to pour in. The investigators' file noted that over two hundred leads had been followed up on in the week following Rosario's disappearance. Some were routine, others bizarre. Without going into detail, an anonymous letter from a psychic to West Miami police said that Rosario could be found somewhere west of Miami. Another said Rosario was alive, while a third said she was probably alive and standing in water somewhere in the Florida Everglades.

On Wednesday, March 3, police got a more ominous lead. A motorist driving the Pompano Turnpike Monday night glanced to the side of the road and saw a young woman in red shorts run from a car stopped at the Pompano Turnpike Plaza. Two men caught her and beat her back into the car. When they drove off, the motorist followed them to the Boca Raton turnoff, where he lost them. He said they were driving a Chevrolet sedan, with a Florida license plate bearing the digits 378.

Wasserman called the Department of Motor Vehicles in Tallahassee and requested a computer printout of all cars bearing that partial tag number. It took over an hour for the computer to spit out the 12,000 names with those numbers in the registration, with 1,000 for Chevrolets.

The detectives focused on those owners who lived in the Dade County area and who had police records. They were still at it when two Canadian psychics showed up at the police station on March 6 and announced they could help find Rosario. Poring over a map of Dade County, they led Detective Morin and Sergeant Bobby Cheatam across a large section of west Homestead, pointing out abandoned houses, wells, and ditches. The detectives checked out the abandoned houses, wells, and ditches, but found no sign of the girl. The Canadian psychics returned to Miami Beach for sun while the detectives went back to their work.

On Sunday, March 11, Detective George Morin was in the homicide-detail office of the Miami police station, going through the names on the computer printout, when he got a call from a private investigator, Ken Whittaker.

"What can I do for you?" Morin asked gruffly. He and Detective Harvey Wasserman had worked more hours than they cared to remember on the Gonzalez case and they were in no mood to chitchat with a Miami gumshoe.

Whittaker, however, wasn't interested in talking shop. He told Morin about the Beth Kenyon disappearance. Christopher Wilder was the suspect. Wilder was also a racing enthusiast and had been at the Miami Grand Prix on the weekend Rosario Gonzalez disappeared.

Whittaker saw a connection. Two pretty young women, both about the same age and similar in appearance, had disappeared in the Miami area within a week of each other under mysterious circumstances. Both knew Wilder, a convicted sex offender. Now both were gone.

Whittaker offered a theory—both girls had been kidnapped by the same man, Christopher Wilder. Morin liked the theory. He thanked the private eye for the tip, hung up, and called the Gonzalez home. He asked Mrs. Gonzalez if she knew anyone by the name of Christopher Wilder.

The mother thought for a moment. "I don't think so," she replied.

Morin called Metro Dade homicide and asked to talk to the detective handling the Kenyon case. A few minutes later a Metro Dade detective got on the line and said no one had been assigned to the case. It was still buried in missing persons.

On Monday morning, March 12, Miami Detective Harvey Wasserman got a call from Coral Gables Police Officer Mitch Fry. On his own, Fry had also reached the conclusion that Chris Wilder was behind the disappearance of the two Miami-area girls.

Wasserman recalled the conversation: "All of a sudden all the hairs on the back of your neck stand up on end and you get a cold chill."

Fry had taken the file to the Miami police because Metro Dade refused to investigate.

Wasserman called a detective he knew in the Palm Beach County Sheriff's Office and asked for a rundown on Wilder. The answer was chilling.

"The guy is a psycho," the Palm Beach detective said. "He's capable of anything."

Wasserman's next call was to the Metro Dade Public Safety Department. It did the trick, because Beth Kenyon's missing persons report was kicked upstairs to the homicide detail and assigned to a team of detectives.

Wasserman felt very good about the turn of events. "We had something to work," he said. "We all felt that Christopher Wilder was going to be our guy."

Chapter Seven

If the sudden interest in his personal life by Miami detectives bothered Christopher Wilder, it didn't show. He still went to DJ's diner in Boynton Beach each morning for breakfast, where he bantered with the smiling counter waitress while wolfing down his steak and eggs. He still took his daily swim in the pool or at the beach. He still swung by the Sawtel offices in the afternoon, where he passed the time shuffling contracts and making phone calls. And he still went to the posh nightclubs from Palm Beach to Fort Lauderdale, looking for pretty, available women, buying them drinks, and perhaps taking them to dinner. A few people at the office had started to wonder why private eyes were snooping around—but not Chris. At least not outwardly.

* * *

On Thursday, March 8, Wilder saw his Palm Beach County probation officer on a routine visit and after a brief chat stopped by his seamstress to have his black racing suit monogrammed.

The seamstress happened to be the wife of a Palm Beach police detective, Tom Neighbors, a casual friend of Wilder's who shared a common interest in racing. Neighbors was home, and the two chatted briefly about the upcoming twenty-four-hour endurance race at Sebring, which Wilder had entered.

"He was pretty excited about the race," Neighbors said, recalling their pleasant, if brief, conversation.

Wilder also kept his appointment with the person who perhaps knew him best, sex therapist Ginger Bush. He had been seeing her since being referred by the South County Mental Health Association in 1979. Wilder rarely missed an appointment. He was plagued by violent fantasies and periodic blackouts, and admitted if it weren't for the psychiatric help, he would have gone off the deep end years ago.

Wilder's sex problems surfaced in Australia, where he grew up a nervous, lonely schoolboy who bit his nails until they bled.

"The bloke was a bit standoffish, but didn't seem like a madman or anything like that," is how a school chum later remembered him.

At age seventeen, Wilder and some other teenagers cornered a girl on the beach after school. Wilder approached her and said he would keep the others away if she had sex with him. The girl did, and afterward the others raped her while Wilder watched.

The youths were arrested for gang rape, and Wilder was forced to undergo psychiatric treatment, which included group-therapy sessions and electric-shock treatments.

The electric shock apparently had a lasting effect, for when he grew older, Wilder had fantasies in which he administered electric shock to women while having sex with them.

The therapist told Miami detectives that Wilder had an obsession to physically and mentally dominate women and to turn them into slaves who would do everything he asked them to. He also was drawn toward such subjects as white slavery and said he fantasized about holding a woman captive against her will.

One of his favorite books was *The Collector*, the tale of a clerk and butterfly collector in England who becomes wealthy and nets his finest specimen, a twenty-year-old art student. He kidnaps the woman, holds her captive on his estate, and forces her to pose for photographs.

It was Wilder's favorite book. He kept several copies at the house and had read the book so many times he could recite paragraphs from memory. He also saw the movie, which starred Samantha Eggar—a former English model in her twenties with long brown hair that fell past her shoulders.

Wilder told the therapist of his *Collector* fantasies, of wanting to dominate women, of wanting complete power over them. The therapist knew of Wilder's past record, his dark thoughts. And she knew, from a *Miami Herald* story, about the missing Rosario

Gonzalez. She asked at one of their last sessions if he knew anything about the missing model.

Wilder looked her straight in the eye. "I read that too, and I can tell you I had nothing to do with it."

"He was as cool as a cucumber," she later told police. "I had my doubts, but he didn't bat an eye."

If Wilder was cucumber cool, his partner, L. K. Kimbrell, was not. Five years earlier he had started Sawtel Electric with someone he thought he knew, but now he wasn't so sure.

After the business got going, Wilder stopped coming to the office, much to Kimbrell's regret. A silent partner is how Kimbrell now described him: a guy who shows up regularly only to collect his check.

Kimbrell knew about his partner's flashy, *Playboy* life-style. That was okay; the guy was a bachelor and what he did in his private life was his own business. He did find it amusing that Wilder was seen as a millionaire. Kimbrell signed the checks, and he knew how much Wilder made. He also knew how his partner operated. The bachelor pad on Mission Hill Road had been a dump that Wilder bought for $60,000 and had remodeled with tailings and leftovers picked up from Sawtel Construction. The white Porsche 911 Carrera that he drove and the charcoal-gray Cadillac were both several years old. Even the two flashy rings with the teardrop-size five-carat diamonds Wilder liked to flash before dates were actually zircons, worth maybe $400 at the most.

All flash and no cash. And that was okay too. If Wilder put on airs, well, he wasn't the first to do so in Florida. These things didn't bother Kimbrell, but the sex arrests—they were something else. That was sick.

When Wilder returned from Australia in January, Kimbrell asked what had happened.

"It was a big screwup," Wilder said. "Those girls wanted me to take those pictures. I didn't know they were fifteen, they told me they were twenty."

Then Kimbrell wanted to know what had happened to Beth Kenyon, and about the alibi Wilder worked out with the secretary before the private eyes arrived. The alibi had been Wilder's idea: he wanted the secretary to lie for him.

"Do you know what happened to her?" Kimbrell asked.

Wilder shook his head. "There's a guy who says he saw me with Beth at a gas station. But the guy has me mixed up with somebody else. I haven't seen Beth since we had dinner a month ago. I told them that, but they won't believe me. I don't know why they want to pin this thing on me."

Kimbrell wanted to believe him. Wilder didn't seem like a psycho. He was the type of guy who blushed when fellow workers used profanity or graphic language in describing sex acts. He had worked with women in the office and no one had ever complained. Many of the women liked him, in fact; he was polite and courteous and always said hello.

Miami police and Metro Dade detectives were investigating the disappearance of the two aspiring models, but the FBI was still reluctant to get involved.

William Kenyon had called the Bureau's Miami office after it was apparent Metro Dade was pursuing the missing persons report but was told the FBI could not investigate because there was no proof of kidnapping. "Why don't you try Metro Dade?" the investigator suggested.

Metro Dade was making progress. Five investigators had been put on the Kenyon case since it was turned over to homicide on Monday. Most of their time was spent on interviewing witnesses and verifying information already ferreted out by the private detectives and off-duty patrol officer Mitch Fry. They had shown a photo lineup to the gas station attendant who last saw Beth Kenyon. And lab technicians had gone over Beth's sporty Chrysler, which was found at Miami International Airport. And they had questioned persons who had seen Wilder just days before her disappearance. One person they did not talk to was Christopher Wilder himself.

"What was the point?" Detective Ray Nazario said later to a reporter. "There was no evidence available at the time to suggest any criminal activity or foul play. There was no crime at this point. I couldn't accuse him of abduction. I could bring him back here and put him under the lights, but this is 1984 and we don't do that sort of thing."

Wilder had told Ken Whittaker Senior that he was willing to appear in a standup lineup. But that idea, for the time being, was nixed by Metro Dade detectives.

"You can't do that," Detective Nazario said. "First of all, Wilder would have to volunteer to us, and I'm certain that he would have contacted an attorney who would have said, 'Forget it!' And if the station attendant did say, 'Yes, that's the guy who paid for Miss Kenyon's gas,' what do we do to him then? Put him in jail for forty years? There's no crime in paying for a beautiful girl's gas.''

Metro Dade did learn Wilder had violated his parole when he left Palm Beach County to go race at the Miami Grand Prix on Saturday, February 25. But the detectives did not pick up Wilder for parole violation.

''In a homicide investigation you have to be methodical and discount nothing,'' Nazario said. ''In this business you don't deal with only the deceased but with the life of the potential subject—because he could get the electric chair for first-degree murder. There is nothing you can do first. We had no proof that he was a maniac. Nobody had reason to believe Mr. Wilder was anybody but a hardworking businessman known to Elizabeth Kenyon and her family.''

Meanwhile, a lead surfaced in the Rosario Gonzalez disappearance that sent a hot shot of adrenaline through the detectives working the case. A man had called the Gonzalez family early Tuesday morning and said he was holding their daughter prisoner and would release her if they came up with $10,000 ransom.

''No tricks,'' he warned. ''Get me the money and the girl goes unhurt.''

Ten detectives were assigned to ferreting out the kidnapper. The phone was tapped and the parents' Homestead home watched. An FBI agent was also called in for assistance.

When the kidnapper called again, he was kept on the phone while the call was traced. Fifteen minutes later lawmen surrounded a fading apartment complex in South Miami and arrested an eighty-year-old man who was the great-grandfather of the missing girl. After being held, he was later freed on bond. He had no idea where the girl was. "He was lonely," a police officer said. "He wanted attention."

The same day Beth's mother called the FBI to plead again for assistance in finding their daughter. The FBI again refused; since there was no extortion plot, an agent told her, the Bureau had no legal jurisdiction in the case.

The rebuff might have stopped the average person, but not William Kenyon. Kenyon was a prosperous businssman with a string of supermarkets in upstate New York. He had political clout and knew how to use it. And when the FBI again turned him down, he got on the phone. Soon the FBI received calls from New York Congressman John J. LaFalce, Senator Alfonse D'Amato, and Wisconsin Governor Lee Sherman Dreyfus, all insisting the FBI get off the dime and start investigating.

On Wednesday, March 14, the FBI quietly and unofficially entered the case. They offered assistance to the Metro Dade detectives and checked out 190 leads that were outside Dade County. They obtained psychiatric examinations and records of Wilder's three arrests on sex charges. They questioned state parole officer Rick Erwin and questioned friends who had seen Wilder the day following Beth's disappearance. They did everything except question Christopher

Wilder. "We didn't anticipate talking to him at that stage of the game," said Joe del Campo, spokesman for the FBI office in Miami.

Nobody bothered to watch him either—not the FBI, Metro Dade, or the Palm Beach police or sheriff. For the eight days following the discovery that the thirty-eight-year-old race car driver was the last one to see Beth alive, he was allowed to come and go as he pleased, living out his *Playboy* fantasy, or getting rid of bodies or evidence.

On Tuesday, March 13, Christopher Wilder celebrated his thirty-ninth birthday. The day before, as a present to himself, he bought a 1973 Chrysler New Yorker. Unlike the Eldorado and cream-colored Porsche, or the other ten vehicles at his disposal, the New Yorker lacked flashy style; it was just a functional late-model sedan, designed to lug the family around. It did the job with little fanfare. It was a prosaic vehicle that blended into the background and would never catch a second glance.

It was just what Wilder wanted: the perfect getaway car.

Chapter Eight

In mid-March spring broke on the Florida south coast like a thunderous wall of emerald green churned up by an offseason hurricane. In this case, the green was cash as students by the tens of thousands left colleges and universities in the chilly East and Midwest and swept southeast for a week or so of fun in the sun.

The tollways and interstates were bumper to bumper, and the airlines booked to capacity. In Washington, Congress debated whether the economy was on the upswing or in an inflationary period, but the hordes converging upon the beach towns from Daytona to Miami couldn't care less. Those that had money flaunted it; those that didn't borrowed, and occasionally stole.

Unlike some years past, the weather was perfect,

and the merchants were ready. Bars and restaurants with only a decent location stood to make as much profit in a day as they did in a week during summer. The same went for liquor store owners and motel operators, who jumped the rate of a room five times.

The spring hordes didn't care about the gouging and found ways to cope. In Daytona Beach, an unofficial gathering spot for motorcycle gangs, bikers drank their beer on the beach and skipped motel costs by taking speed. In Fort Lauderdale enterprising natives rented cabins by the week, then sublet sleeping space on the floors at $5 a head. In Miami students stayed in trailer and RV parks west of the city or slept under blankets in their cars and hoped the cops didn't notice.

New Orleans had its Mardi Gras and South Florida had spring break; both were traditions as old as time itself, or at least 1962 when "Where The Boys Are" was made. The 1984 remake was in the movie houses, but no one was watching, as the boys were too busy ogling girls at the Elbow Room's wet T-shirt night, or the no T-shirt night that had become a popular spring ritual on the beach.

When it was over, they returned to Georgia Tech and the University of Michigan, their blistered skin covered with Noxema as they dreamed of the nifty sorority girls they almost scored with. No one remembered the stomachaches from too much fast food, or the gouging they took at every turn. This was spring break, and dreams were not made of such mundane stuff.

With so much going on, few paid attention to the March 16 story that appeared in the *Miami Herald* of the Boynton Beach race car driver wanted for questioning in the disappearance of two South Florida women. The article did not name the suspect, but described him as a wealthy contractor and gave a physical description.

Several residents of Boynton Beach's Mission Hill Road took the *Herald*, but no one connected the man in the story with their neighbor, Christopher Wilder, even though Wilder had a playboy reputation and drove race cars.

"Mr. Wilder was always so nice," a female resident said. "It just never occurred to us."

But others, including some of his racing friends, made the connection, and they found it hard to believe.

On Thursday, the day after the story appeared, Wilder missed his appointment with his sex therapist. He also failed to show up at Sawtel Construction that afternoon.

He wasn't at home. The Cadillac and the Porsche were locked in the garage, the lights were off, and the three English setters were inside, barking when strangers approached.

On Friday Wilder telephoned his partner, Kimbrell, at Sawtel Construction. "I'm in Tallahassee," Wilder said. "I've run into some problems."

Kimbrell asked what kind of problems, but Wilder refused to go into it.

"Look, get back here," Kimbrell urged. "You haven't done anything that can't be straightened out."

Wilder returned to Boynton Beach that evening at ten o'clock. Kimbrell had never seen his business partner so distraught. Wilder was in tears. The cops are after me, he said. They want to frame me for Beth's disappearance. I don't know anything about it but the cops don't care. They just want a fall guy, somebody to take the rap.

"I am not going to jail," he cried. "I am not going to do it."

No one followed Chris Wilder home that night. If they had done so, they would have seen Wilder take his three English setters to the kennel he jointly owned in Fort Lauderdale. Then they would have seen him put a suitcase in his recently purchased Chrysler and bid farewell to his business partner.

Had Wilder been stopped and his car searched, they would have found a loaded .357 revolver, spare ammunition, handcuffs, a roll of duct tape, rope, a sleeping bag, a copy of John Fowles's *The Collector*, and a fifteen-foot length of electric cord that had been slit down the middle and fitted with a special switch.

Had he been stopped then, his "travelogue of terror" would have never begun.

Chapter Nine

Two hours north of Boynton Beach lies Indian Harbour, a sleepy beach town that is busy only on humid weekends and during the manned spacecraft launches from Cape Canaveral, twelve miles to the north.

Unhurried and slow moving, this town of six thousand was, until recently, a place of modest slab homes owned by hardworking middle-class folk—a beach town for people who couldn't afford to live at the beach.

Terry Ferguson was born on Cape Cod but moved to Indian Harbour with her mother at the age of one. Now twenty-one and a willowy, brown-eyed brunette, she had graduated from Satellite High School in 1981 and landed a job with World Class, Inc., a local

T-shirt printing company. When she joined the
company, it had just 8 employees. Three years later
it had 120, and back orders that kept the silk-screening
plant opened seven days a week.

"Terry was the second person hired," recalled
company Vice President Scott Reardon. "She was
one of the people that really made the company. She
was ambitious and wanted to grow with us and move
up in the company."

Terry wasn't sure that was what she wanted to do.
With her boyfriend, Dan Bednarz, or at her parents',
at their Indian Harbour beach home, she often talked
about a career in fashion modeling. It was not exactly
a passing fantasy for a sinewy young woman who
stood five feet, seven inches tall, weighed 115 pounds,
and possessed a pretty, angular face that could look
haunted, alluring, or plain squeaky clean with just a
touch of makeup.

Friends had remarked how she was pretty enough
to make the big time, and though Terry blushed when
she heard such compliments, deep inside she felt they
just might be right. She had also given thought to
leaving Florida.

Her boyfriend had given her a diamond promise
ring, and they were kicking around the idea of moving to Connecticut after he graduated from Florida
Institute of Technology. Terry planned attending the
Wilford Beauty Academy while Bednarz tried landing
a marketing job with a New York firm.

And if that didn't work out, Terry had also given
thought to a cosmetology career. She had always had
a thousand different ideas, her mother recalled. She

was always doing something, going somewhere, on the move. Her life was bright with promise—until fate cut it short.

Terry had promised herself that March to go to Fort Lauderdale for a weekend and catch some of the spring break fun. She planned to go with Sandra "Sam" Knowles, a nineteen-year-old college student from Simpco, Ontario, Canada who was on semester break. Sandra was staying with her sister Jeanne Edders, a co-worker at the T-shirt plant and a friend of Terry's.

The girls planned to rendezvous with Terry's boyfriend, Dan Bednarz, who was leaving for Fort Lauderdale on Friday afternoon with a buddy from Connecticut. The girls would stay until early Saturday morning, when they would return to Indian Harbour so Terry could go to work.

The trip, however, never materialized. Terry's boss had decided to give her and the other employees Saturday off by having them work on Sunday instead of Saturday. "It was spring break," he reasoned, "and everyone wanted to party." But employees complained that they had already made plans for Sunday and wanted to work the normal Saturday evening shift. "So I dropped the idea," he said. "It wasn't fair to the others to change on short notice."

Terry had to work and Sandra decided not to go alone, so it meant both girls would be stuck close to home, at least for that weekend.

Friday evening Terry went to Dan's apartment to see him off to Fort Lauderdale. Dan could see she was upset and promised her that he would be back

Sunday morning so they could have their Sunday breakfast at the Blueberry Muffin Restaurant in Indialantic.

"I'm going to keep you to that," she said, kissing Dan good night.

Saturday morning Terry's mother, Frances, and stepfather Don Ferguson, an Indian Harbour police captain, woke their daughter to tell her they were going golfing.

"We never left the house without letting each other know where we were going and when we would be back," Mrs. Ferguson said.

At three that afternoon Terry arrived at World Class, Inc., to spend the next eight hours checking T-shirt designs for defects and placing them in bins. First a snow skiing design, then an island scene, a waterskier slaloming, and "Spring Break 1984" rolled off the press that night.

After work Terry and her friend Sam Knowles went to celebrate St. Patrick's Day at Bennigan's, a bar in nearby Melbourne. It was a glitzy place with Victorian-style decor and stained-glass windows and with waiters and waitresses not much older than Terry, dressed up in green vests and sleeve garters. While there they met one of Terry's co-workers, Kirsten Hansen, and at 12:35 A.M. the group ventured to Jubilation, a fashionable disco at the Holiday Inn oceanfront hotel in Indialantic, east of Melbourne.

It was one of Terry's favorite places to go dancing. But not this night. At 1:30 A.M. Terry told Sam she had spotted an old boyfriend with another woman and wanted to leave.

Sam understood. "It hurt Terry to see him with someone else."

But Sam was not ready to leave and said she would catch a ride home with one of her friends. Before leaving, the three girls agreed to go shopping the next morning.

Terry jumped into the 1977 Pontiac Sunbird and headed back for Indian Harbour alone. At two that morning Frances Ferguson saw a light on in the living room and found Terry curled up in a hair chair reading a book by her favorite author, Stephen King.

Mrs. Ferguson said good night and promised to wake her daughter up in the morning so she could get some sun before going shopping. The following morning Terry rose early and went in the backyard to work on her tan and read her Stephen King novel. At eleven A.M. she slipped into a burgundy blouse, blue jeans, and boots. Before leaving she poked her head into the bathroom where her mother was taking a shower and told her she would be back in a few hours. It was the last time Terry would speak to her mother.

She stopped by to pick up her two friends to go shopping. But Kirsten had spent a long morning at Jubilation and didn't feel up to it and Sam had gone to a doctor that morning after getting hit in the eye with a football.

Terry scribbled her friend a note before leaving for the mall: "Shame on you for not calling me. Hope you get better. I'll see you tomorrow at work. Terry."

Terry arrived at the Merritt Square Mall shortly before one P.M., parking her 1977 Pontiac Sunbird near the J. C. Penney's. Several persons remembered seeing the pretty, aspiring model going from store to store. She was alone, they recalled.

Dan Bednarz returned from his weekend of fun in Fort Lauderdale Sunday afternoon to take Terry out for a late breakfast at the waffle house. He was disappointed when Mrs. Ferguson told him Terry was out shopping; he had hoped to see her. He called back at two o'clock, but Terry still had not arrived. By five that afternoon he was calling every half hour. Figuring she had met a friend at the mall and gone for a drink, he started looking for her—at T.G.I. Friday's, then Bennigan's and Jubilation. She was not at those places and no one had seen her.

At 10:30 P.M. her stepfather drove out to the shopping mall and began searching the nearly empty parking lot. Near the J. C. Penney's, he found Terry's Sunbird. The doors were locked and inside were the blouse and blue jeans that Terry had worn when she left home. Dan Bednarz joined Ferguson at the car. The police captain went home at midnight, but Bednarz stayed with her car until 4:30 that morning, when he finally went home.

At 9:30 Monday morning, Frances Ferguson went to Kirsten Hansen's home, convinced her daughter had spent the night there. Terry hadn't. Terry also had not contacted Sam Knowles, who had returned from the doctor to find Terry's hastily written note. Sam was as concerned as the Fergusons were about Terry's unexplained absence. It was so unlike her to go somewhere without telling her folks.

At three that afternoon Captain Ferguson paid a visit to the World Class, Inc., offices, hoping that his daughter might show up to begin her shift. She didn't, and no one knew where she was.

Meanwhile, an investigation into Terry's disappearance was begun by the shopping mall security police, under the direction of Lieutenant Jerry Jones. After questioning seventy clerks who were working Sunday, Jones determined Terry had entered or been seen in front of three shops that Sunday afternoon. He learned Terry had purchased a shirt at a boutique in one store and had carried it out in a bag. She was last seen walking out of the store in the middle of the mall at about 2:30 P.M. wearing her burgundy shirt, jeans, and boots.

No one saw her go back to her car, where her clothes were found, or saw anyone approach her. It was possible that she was kidnapped, but Jones thought it unlikely. The mall traffic was light on that Sunday, and the clerks were trained to spot and report any instances of people bothering shoppers.

Authorities figured she had changed into the new clothes she bought at the mall, then returned to her car and tossed the clothes she had been wearing into the back seat. What they didn't know is what happened after that.

About an hour after Terry was last seen at the shopping mall, the Texaco gas station in Cocoa Beach, ten miles south of Melbourne, got a call from a man wanting a tow.

"My damn car is stuck in the sand," he said.

He gave as his location a spot off state road AIA, near the Canaveral Groves. A sly flicker of a smile crossed the driver's face as he pulled off the road and into a grove of trees where the Chrysler New Yorker was hubcap deep in sand. The tow truck knew the place well. It was a lover's lane where high school kids took their dates after the movies.

The man who called for the tow truck was a bit old for high school—the driver figured him to be in his mid- or late thirties, with light blonde hair that was almost bald on top and a full, neatly clipped beard— and there was no girl in the car.

"I'm new around here," the man explained after his car was pulled free. "I got sidetracked and then my car sunk here in the sand."

He handed the driver the credit card with L. K. Kimbrell's name on it and let him write up the charge. Afterward, he waved good-bye, got behind the wheel of the Chrysler, and headed north toward the Cape.

"The guy was nice and friendly," the driver later told police. "I'm certain there was no girl in the back seat, but I never did look in the trunk."

On Friday, March 23, the Fergusons got the worst news of their lives; the body of a young woman had been found in Polk County about seventy miles west of Indian Harbour. From the description it sounded like Terry.

Two days earlier a Tampa Electric Company crew was working on the electrical line north of Haines

City, six miles off U.S. 27. One of the workers had climbed a pole to connect an electrical line when he turned around and saw a body floating facedown in the snake-infested creek.

Polk County sheriff's detectives were called to the scene, and the body was fished from the greenish waters. The victim was a young woman in her early twenties, wearing a pink blouse over a tank-top blouse and Calvin Klein jeans. On her left hand was a small diamond ring. Her body had been in the creek for three or four days.

Polk County police checked missing persons. When nothing turned up, they sent out a statewide bulletin that was picked up on the Indian Harbour telex. Detectives from the Brevard County Sheriff's Office drove to Polk County and through dental charts, identified the victim as the missing Terry Ferguson.

The senseless slaying was a front-page story in the small beach towns south of Cape Canaveral.

"She was a very beautiful girl, very attractive," her stepfather told the local paper, *Today*. "She was liked by a lot of people, everyone. She was conscientious. I used to get angry when she called us to tell us where she was at one or two in the morning. Now I'd give anything for her to call."

Frances Ferguson called her daughter "my best friend. We had kind of a sister relationship. She never brought me one bit of grief."

Police spent the better part of two days wading in the chest-high waters of the swamp creek and searching the muddy embankments for evidence. But clues were hard to come by.

The creek runs under a bridge on Deenstill Road, a dirt road running east-west between U.S. 27 and State 33, north of Polk City. The killer could have been from the surrounding area, or he might have just been passing through.

About the only solid lead police had surfaced when a woman said she had seen Terry in the shopping mall on Sunday, talking to a man with light brown hair and a beard and wearing a camera around his neck.

When FBI agents talked to the woman a few days later, they showed her a photo lineup of six men matching the general description. The witness did not hesitate. "That's him," she said, pointing to the mug shot of Christopher Wilder. "That's the man I saw in the shopping center."

Chapter Ten

For the better part of a week Christopher Wilder was little more than a name included in an investigation file that had been given low priority by the FBI office in Miami. The rape-torture of the Tennessee coed in the Georgia motel changed that. After Wilder was identified in the photo lineup, the case was given top-priority status.

The FBI suspected Wilder might head west toward California, or possibly north to New York. It seemed unlikely he would return to Florida, where he was wanted for the kidnapping of the Tallahassee coed and suspected in the disappearances of two South Florida women.

But Wilder proved to be unpredictable. Wednesday morning he returned to the shopping center where he had abducted the girl and found her car still parked in the lot. Using her keys, which he took from her in the motel, he drove to a bar a few blocks away, where he spent an hour chatting with a cocktail waitress and sipping a drink. When the bar closed, he drove the car to a bank across the street from the mall and left it.

Tallahassee police were at a loss to explain Wilder's action. They figured he probably left town in the late model white Chrysler that he had used in the kidnapping, since it did not turn up during a search of the mall or the streets near the bar.

Interstate 10 snakes through the Gulf Coast states, a white ribbon of cement slinking through the green cotton fields of Mississippi and swampy bayous of Louisiana before it enters the pine tree country of eastern Texas.

Beaumont is just over the line from Louisiana, where Interstate 10 connects with Highway 96. An odd mix of southern gentility and Texas can do-ism. Beaumont was home to Terry Diane Walden, a twenty-four-year-old nursing student at nearby Lamar University.

Daughter of a local auctioneer and copper buyer, Terry grew up in this city of 100,000 and attended Forest Park High School. She grew into a pretty blonde with hazel eyes, who carried just 105 pounds on a five-foot four-inch frame, and according to a friend, "carried it well." With her clear, all-American looks and flare for fashion, some thought Terry might gravitate toward the high-fashion world of Houston, sixty miles to the south.

But the temptations of the Lone Star State's biggest and wealthiest city did not appeal to the shy, sensitive small-town girl. Deep down, she was a small-town woman, who enjoyed the simple pleasures of going to a movie at the local theater, or a weekend water skiing on the Neches River.

After graduating from high school in 1978, she married John David Walden, a handsome Goodyear Chemical employee, who had gone to the same high school. Two years later they became the parents of a daughter, Mindy. The family quickly grew to four when Sabrina, a daughter by John's previous marriage, came to live with them the next year.

The court had awarded them custody of the cherub-faced nine-year-old after a grueling battle in which Terry staunchly supported her husband. Terry was content to be a housewife. Then she had decided to return to school and enrolled in the nursing program at Lamar.

The classes cut into the time she could spend with her family, but Terry was immersed in the nursing program.

"She had a feeling of purpose," a friend recalled. "She really felt it was important to help people, and this was a way to do it. She was working with patients at St. Elizabeth Hospital, and that was all she talked about."

Friday, March 23, began no differently than any other weekday. Rising early she made breakfast for her family, then drove four-year-old Mindy to the

Baby Redbird Day Care Center before heading for the university campus. Had this been just another Friday, Terry would have finished with her classes by that afternoon and returned to pick up Mindy to arrive back home in time to see nine-year-old Sabrina return home from school. Instead, the day ended with her husband going to the Beaumont Police Department to fill out a missing persons report on his wife.

He told the night-shift officer that he had feared for his wife's safety after she failed to pick up their daughter from the day-care center.

"She would never do anything like that," he explained to the officer.

The police treated the report routinely—looking over accident reports, calling area hospitals, but no one matching Terry's description had been in an accident or had been admitted to a hospital emergency room.

Over the weekend detectives determined to their satisfaction that the beautiful twenty-four-year-old mother of two had not left home for personal reasons. She loved her husband and two children, and had a budding nursing career she very much wanted to pursue. There was no reason for her to leave.

The husband told police that Terry had driven to school in the 1981 burnt-orange Mercury Cougar which he had recently purchased from his sister. The car was Terry's pride and joy—"She was in heaven driving that car," her sister-in-law said—and she always parked it in the campus lot near her classes. The car was not there when her husband went to look for it.

A friend said she saw Terry before 11:30 A.M., Friday, as she walked through the Lamar University Setzer Student Center. Terry had books in her hands and was in a hurry, as if she was late for class, the friend recalled. She appeared to be alone.

The whereabouts of the missing coed remained a mystery through the weekend. The family was advised to keep close to the telephone in case Terry called, and the city's patrol officers were told to keep an eye peeled for the burnt-orange Cougar that Terry had driven to the university. Then at eight o'clock Monday morning, an employee with the Lower Neches Valley Authority was checking a canal dam on the west side of the city when he noticed a bright object floating in the sluggish waters. The object was a pink lady's jacket. As he went to retrieve the garment, he saw something else—the body of a fully clothed woman, floating facedown in the water.

Investigators from the Jefferson County Sheriff's Office and the Beaumont Police Department rushed to the scene to begin a joint investigation. Forty detectives were involved in the case by late afternoon, questioning witnesses and searching the muddy canal banks and tree-studded fields for clues.

Terry's body was taken to the Galveston County Hospital at Texas City for the autopsy, which was performed by medical examiner Dr. W. E. Korndorffer. It was initially thought the woman had been shot, because empty shell casings were found along the west bank. The autopsy, however, revealed that Terry had not been shot and had died from a massive blood loss caused by multiple stab wounds. Korndorffer found three stab wounds to the chest and an exit wound in the back. The knife thrusts caused cuts to the lungs, heart, and left pulmonary artery, with the wounds to the chest being delivered with such force that they fractured two of her ribs.

The medical examiner found three types of rope with the body, including a venetian blind cord and a half inch of nylon rope. There were also adhesive marks on her face, indicating her mouth had been taped shut.

"She was tied up when she was stabbed," the medical examiner told Beaumont Police Lieutenant Charles Henderson. "Then the ropes were untied and she was put in the canal."

He said Terry had been dead for several days and probably had been slain within hours after she dropped off her daughter.

"There was no evidence of sexual assault or torture," the medical examiner said. "But I can't rule out the possibility that that didn't happen."

The search of the crime scene continued well into Monday afternoon. Scuba divers searched the murky waters of the five-foot-deep canal by hand, while a spotter plane on loan from the Texas Rangers office in Houston swept the skies. The massive search turned up a set of shoe prints leading to and from the west bank of the canal near the spot where the body was sighted. A piece of silver duct tape, believed to be used to seal the young woman's mouth, was found on the muddy bank. Also found were a set of tire tracks that led up to a farm road that connected with U.S. 90. The detectives worked on the theory that the young woman had been killed near the canal bank where the body was found.

"It's an isolated area, and there's a road that runs along the canal that a car could travel easily and not be seen from," a sheriff's investigator told a reporter from the *Beaumont Enterprise*. "We have talked to some people who have been very helpful."

The identity of the person who traveled that dirt road with the young mother of two possibly tied up in the back seat or trunk remained a mystery. Terry's husband, however, was able to provide a clue. He said two days before her disappearance Terry had come home from her classes and said that a man posing as a photographer had pestered her that day.

"She told me about this guy who came up while she was walking across campus and asked if she was interested in modeling," John told police. "She said she thanked him for his interest but turned down the offer and kept walking."

The man followed her and suggested they go to his car, where he had a briefcase with samples of his work.

"Terry told me she just laughed, called him some kind of pervert, and told him to leave her alone."

A friend of Terry's walked up and the man hurriedly left. John Walden asked Terry what the man looked like and she told him he was wearing a suit and had a beard. She said he was in his mid- or late thirties and looked too old to be a student. Terry didn't mention the incident again, and John forgot about it until her body was found in the canal.

"It just didn't seem that important," he said.

The statement was hastily scribbled into a notebook and later typed up that evening into a single-spaced police report. It was added to the pile of other reports that had been collected. Its significance was not learned for almost a week.

Far more pressing was the recovery of the burnt-orange Mercury Cougar. An all-points bulletin was sent to law enforcement agencies in the South and Southwest with a vehicle description and the Texas license number.

"We need to find that car badly," Jefferson County Sheriff's Captain Jack Brown told assembled reporters at a press conference on March 29. "It may hold information which will get us headed toward a solid path in the investigation."

Dozens of citizens, shocked by the senseless murder, called the Crimestopper hotline offering tips. An employee at the Parkdale Mall told police he saw a woman matching Terry Walden's description walking by shops about noon Friday. She was alone and was apparently shopping. Two others called to report seeing a man and a woman fitting Terry's description in a car similar to the missing Cougar south of the canal about eight o'clock Friday evening. The informants unfortunately were not close enough to be sure it was Terry, or to identify the man in the car.

The single-page reports piled up until they threatened to spring the three-ring hardcover binder that held them. But despite all the hours of detective work and the help of a community eager to find the young woman's killer, police were unable to find the missing Cougar or produce a suspect.

"We have developed a profile on her now as well as background material on everyone involved," a weary Lieutenant Henderson told the press on March 30. "We have eliminated no one, nor do we have anything that looks like a concrete lead. She was a person who lived for her family and trusted everyone."

Henderson did not tell the assembled reporters about the search for a second car, a search that had begun after a brief all-points bulletin, issued by the FBI, had crossed the department's telex on March 26.

The vehicle was the cream-colored 1973 Chrysler New Yorker purchased a week earlier in Florida and driven by fugitive Christopher Wilder.

The bulletin caught the attention of the task force detectives assigned to the Walden murder. Wilder matched the description of the photographer who had pestered Terry at the Lamar University campus two days before she disappeared. She also was the pretty, vulnerable type of woman that Wilder preyed upon.

The Beaumont lawmen learned from the FBI that Wilder had been spotted in Baton Rouge, Louisiana, on March 21, where it was believed he stole the license plates from a car parked in a motel. The following day a man driving a 1973 Chrysler with the stolen license-plate numbers registered at the Best Western Gulf Coast Motel in Winnie, with a Visa credit card issued to "L. K. Kimbrell."

The manager said the guest checked into the room alone and left the following morning. Agents took the registration card and searched the room. Prints found in the room were determined to be Wilder's.

Winnie is a gas-stop town of 1,500 off Interstate

10, twenty-five miles south of Beaumont. Detectives figured Wilder had been on his way to Houston when for some reason he decided to double back toward Beaumont, where he kidnapped and murdered Terry Walden. Detectives believed Wilder killed Terry, then continued on in one of the cars and ditched the other in Beaumont. But which car? And where was it?

Streets and parking lots near the university and Beaumont shopping center where Terry had been reported seen shopping had been searched repeatedly without luck. Both vehicles and the man who had driven them remained a mystery.

Then at 3:30 in the morning, Friday, April 6, a Beaumont police officer was making a routine patrol of the downtown area when he spotted a cream-colored Chrysler parked in front of the Dryden's Discovery store, on Calder Road. The license plates had been removed, but the vehicle matched the one listed on the "hot sheet" issued at the evening briefing.

The officer pulled alongside and requested a computer check of the DIN number found on the dashboard. A few seconds later he got the answer he had suspected he would: the car was Christopher Wilder's.

Beaumont police were sent to guard the vehicle until FBI technicians could arrive later that morning. A plastic wrap was placed over the car to preserve physical evidence that might be found on the car, then was pushed onto a flatbed truck and taken to the police garage. There it was gone over for prints and vacuumed for hair follicles and other evidence.

Bloodstains found inside indicated Wilder had likely carried the body of at least one woman, and possibly others, in the car before disposing of them. The search did not produce a handgun or the thin-bladed eight-to-ten inch fillet-type knife that had been used to kill Terry Walden.

Police believed the car had been left in front of the store the day of the murder. A store clerk told investigators she noticed the car while coming to work. "It's been there a week or more and I've been intending to call police, but I just never got around to it."

Police believed Wilder switched his license plate to Walden's 1981 Cougar when he made his escape. The car still had not been found, but police had no trouble following the bloody trail of the thirty-nine-year-old fugitive.

Since Terry Walden's murder, a woman had disappeared in Oklahoma City, another was missing in Colorado, and a search for a third was under way in Las Vegas, Nevada.

"Wilder represents a significant danger," said Oliver Chuck Revell, assistant FBI director and the agent in charge of the nationwide manhunt. "He's extremely active, very dangerous, and he's making contacts on an almost daily basis."

Just a few weeks before, Wilder was just another affable playboy, living out a fantasy in an obscure beach town. Now he was a candidate for the FBI's Ten Most Wanted list, and would soon be the target of the largest manhunt in the Bureau's fifty-year history.

Chapter Eleven

Shortly before nine o'clock Saturday evening, March 24, a man in his late thirties, driving a burnt-orange Mercury Cougar with a Louisiana license number checked into a Holiday Inn South in Oklahoma City, paying for his lodging with a credit card in the name of L. K. Kimbrell. He ate dinner in the motel's restaurant, ordering New York steak with all the trimmings. He paid for the meal with cash, left a generous tip, and went back to his room. The following morning he bought gas at a Texaco station near the Penn Square Mall and paid the bill with a credit card.

That afternoon twenty-year-old Suzanne Wendy Logan and her husband of nine months, Brian, left their home on West Finely Road in the Village area of

Oklahoma City, and headed for Reno and Western avenues, where Brian worked at the Save-A-Stop. With a good-bye kiss on the cheek the pretty, English-born blonde then headed for Penn Square Mall, where she planned to pick up a watch she had put on layaway and to browse in a few shops before returning home.

A woman at a refreshment stand remembered seeing a slender, attractive woman buying a soft drink. A clerk at Street's store also remembered a woman matching Suzanne's description looking at some twist beads which she was thinking of buying for her mother. She left the store with the beads and headed across the mall, apparently back to her car and then back to the apartment. But she never made it.

Later that evening Brian went to the Oklahoma Police Department and made out a missing persons report on his wife. He said she had an appointment at four o'clock that afternoon to meet a friend to discuss selling Tupperware. But she did not keep the appointment nor did she return to pick Brian up at the Save-A-Stop. He said there had been no problems in the marriage and he could think of no reason for Suzanne to leave so abruptly.

The police officer who took the information told the worried husband a detective would be given the report and would determine what was to be done.

The following day Suzanne's parents in Tulsa, Oklahoma, called the police, seeking information about their daughter. Had they located Suzanne? Did they have any leads? They were stunned to learn that missing persons detail had determined Suzanne was a runaway and detectives would not be assigned to the case.

"They said that Suzanne had decided to leave her husband and that nothing could be done," her father said later. "They said they weren't going to look for her."

The parents called back at least twice a day to see if they could get the police interested in finding their daughter.

"I know they got kind of tired of me telling him that I knew how he felt," said Sergeant Don Helms of the department's missing persons detail. "There just was not any way to get the point across that unless there's some kind of information that a crime had been committed, there wasn't much we could do."

Oklahoma police received three thousand missing persons reports each year. Only a handful were ever investigated. In the Logan case, Helms said, "One, we didn't know where to look. Two, I didn't have any real reason to pry into her personal affairs. And three, if I had, it would have been a violation of the privacy act."

Although witnesses had last placed Suzanne at the mall and her car was later found parked there, Helms did not consider this reason to upgrade the case as anything more than a runaway.

"It just seemed very, very improbable to me that that aggressive a type of abduction had taken place on an afternoon at the mall," Helms said. "We would have had some witnesses. But everyone we talked to said everything was just as cool as could be.''

With no sign of criminal activity, Helms was prevented from placing the missing woman's name on the National Crime Information Center's computer. She was an adult, she was not mentally or physically handicapped, and she did not meet the computer's criteria.

Brian and Suzanne had discussed the possibility of moving to Dallas, where Suzanne hoped to get a job as a model or fashion designer. She had prepared for her new career by taking modeling lessons at a local agency for three years and compiling a portfolio to show modeling agencies. She also had studied fashion design.

"She was real interested in modeling and designing," Brian told police. "She had even designed her own clothes."

A few hours after Suzanne was reported missing, a man driving an orange Mercury checked into room 30 of the I-35 Inn in Newton, Kansas, a road-stop town 160 miles north of Oklahoma City. He left the next morning before daybreak. No one saw him leave. When the maid went to clean the room, she found the bed had been made, the drinking glasses lined up on the bathroom sink, and the towels hung neatly on the bathroom racks. Only clippings of blonde hair found in the trash indicated the room had been occupied.

Milford Reservoir is the largest body of water in bone-dry Kansas. It is located off Interstate 70, 130 miles northeast of Newton near Manhattan. It is a favorite fishing spot, and there were boats on the water Sunday afternoon despite unseasonably cold weather that had filled the sky with snow the night before and sent temperatures plummeting into the 20s.

At 1:30 that afternoon a fisherman rowed to the south shore, within view of the Corps of Engineers office, when he spotted something wedged beneath a cedar tree. Closer inspection revealed the body of a young woman. She was half naked, and her eyes and face were swollen and bruised. The coroner would later note bite marks on both her breasts and a half dozen tiny puncture wounds on her back, apparently made with the tip of a knife. Her straight blonde hair had been severely cut and her pubic hair shaved. She had been raped, then murdered by a knife shoved into her chest above the left breast. She had been dead less than an hour before her body was discovered.

Because no missing persons report was entered into the NCIC computer it would take ten days to identify the young woman as the missing Suzanne Logan.

That evening Christopher Wilder, registering under his business partner's name, checked into a motel outside of Denver. The next night he stayed in Wheat Ridge, Colorado, and the next night in Rifle, where FBI agents missed catching him by just hours. The following morning he arrived in Grand Junction, Colorado, where he stopped to buy breakfast and get gas before heading for the Mesa Mall.

At around noon a man wearing boots, stylish jeans, and a sweater approached a young woman leaving the Mervyn's department store. He gave her a business card from a Denver modeling agency and said he was looking for a model to pose for a fashion feature he was doing. The woman looked at the photographer and handed him back the card, saying she wasn't interested. He thanked her and disappeared into the crowd.

In quieter moments, perhaps after a day working at the leather shop in the mall, Sheryl Bonaventura wondered what she really wanted to do with her life. College, a career in modeling, even marriage to her high school sweetheart were all possibilities. But deep down, as her mother Sandy would later say, "Sheryl didn't know what she wanted to do."

But, then, a career decision at that point in her life was not so pressing. She was only eighteen, ten months out of high school, and at that young age there was no reason to hurry. The future was bright with promise.

Certainly on the afternoon of March 29 there were more pressing things for the pretty blonde-haired teen-ager to worry about than a career or marriage. There was the car to pack, and the last-minute items to buy for her skiing weekend in Aspen. An accomplished skier, Sheryl loved the sport, but this trip had special meaning because she was going to see her boyfriend, Terry Shanahan, who was attending school out of town.

So it was the immediate future that occupied the young woman's thoughts as she slipped behind the wheel of the Mazda RX-7 and headed out to the mall. She and her best friend had talked about the trip the night before, and Sheryl had barely been able to contain her excitement. It was going to be a great weekend; things just couldn't be any better.

Sheryl was born in Lemoore, California, a speck of a town south of Fresno, where her father, James Bonaventura, was stationed at the Naval Air Station. Three years later, when he left the Navy, the family moved to Farmington, New Mexico, where James Bonaventura landed a job as an oil driller. The family moved again to McPherson, Kansas, when Sheryl was in the seventh grade, then finally to Grand Junction two years later.

While in grade school Sheryl developed into something of a tomboy, who seemed to prefer playing volleyball and baseball over dating boys. That changed in the ninth grade when the Bonaventuras settled in Grand Junction. There she met Terry, and soon he became all Sheryl talked about. The two dated through high school, and when he went away she saw him at every opportunity.

Sheryl's interest in modeling began the same time she started dating Terry. She had posed for a few professional photographers and had given some thought to pursuing a career in modeling. In one recent photo Sheryl is shown in a leotard, leg warmers, and headband, leaning forward with her hands on her knees. Victoria Principal could not have looked any prettier.

Recently she had also considered enrolling at Colorado State University. Her grades in high school were only average, a fact she now regretted, but she felt she had a chance of being accepted. A girlfriend also wanted to go, and the two talked about getting a dorm room together.

But one way or another, however, it looked as if Sheryl would be leaving Grand Junction. Her father, who had traveled to Texas in search of a job, had just telephoned home and said he had been offered work.

"Are we going to move, Daddy?" Sheryl asked him.

"Looks that way," he replied.

The news that the family would be moving again made her sad. Although Sheryl had the ability to adjust to new surroundings, she did not want to leave Grand Junction, which had been home for four years and was where most of her close friends lived.

And friends were important to her. "She was sensitive to her friends' feelings, trying to give them equal attention when one felt passed over for another," said boyfriend, Terry Shanahan.

In high school Sheryl was a popular student who loved to go to the big parties, but who often wound up sitting in a corner talking with a friend. Perhaps her closest friend was Kristal Cesario, an eighteen-year-old senior at Grand Junction High School, who was accompanying her on the ski trip.

Sheryl spent Wednesday night at Kristal's home. The two went to dinner at the Pizza Hut that evening and later stayed up until ten P.M., talking about their upcoming ski trip. The following morning Sheryl rose early to return home to pack her ski equipment and suitcase. At 11:30 she called Kristal to say she was going to the Mesa Mall to buy face cream and wanted to know if Kristal wanted to come along. Kristal said she had things to do at the house to prepare for the trip and would see her at two.

At one o'clock, Sheryl arrived at the mall in her brightly polished Mazda, wearing ski parka, jeans, and cowboy boots capped with silver toes. She ran into Chris Mank, a friend and co-worker, and the two went to the One-of-A-Kind Pizza to have a Coke and talk.

The conversation centered around Sheryl's trip to Aspen and the Mesa Mall leather goods store where the two worked. The store was opening a new outlet in Colorado Springs, and they both had been offered jobs there.

After their brief conversation Sheryl headed toward the Target store to buy her face cream. Mank said goodbye, not realizing she would never see her friend again.

By 3:30 that afternoon, Kristal Cesario waited nervously at home, convinced something had happened to Sheryl.

"I knew something was wrong," she said. "Sheryl would have called."

Kristal called the Bonaventuras, who drove to the mall to search for their daughter. All they found was Sheryl's yellow Mazda RX-7. It was parked near the Mervyn's, with the door unlocked and the sunroof halfway open.

After finding the car and checking with her boyfriend, the Bonaventuras became convinced their daughter had been abducted.

"It was just not like her," her mother, Sandy, realized, a bit frightened. "She had never done anything like that before."

Kristal Cesario was also convinced her best friend had been abducted. "Her sunglasses were in the car, and I know she wouldn't have left them there unless something was wrong, because the sun bothered her eyes."

At eight P.M. Jim Bonaventura arrived at the police station to make out a missing persons report on his daughter. Unlike police in Miami and Oklahoma City, Grand Junction police investigated the missing persons report immediately. Their promptness was spurred by an NCIC computer telex warning law enforcement agencies to be on the lookout for Christopher Wilder.

Police officers called Sheryl's friends and searched the mall. Chris Mank told them she saw Sheryl walking toward the Target store. Another friend came forward with the information that she had been in the mall at about 1:30 and spotted Sheryl sitting in her Mazda, talking to a man standing beside it. The stranger, clean shaven and curly haired, did not fit Wilder's description and police suspected he might have been talking to Sheryl about her sports car, which was brightly polished and had a For Sale sign in the window.

A woman in her early twenties was shopping at the mall at noon when a man approached her. He told her he was a photographer and was in search of a young, blue-eyed "cowgirl" type to do some modeling. He offered a business card, indicating he was with an agency in Denver. The woman told police she thought the offer was suspicious and had turned him down cold.

Police showed her an eight-picture photographic

lineup of men with thinning blonde hair and beards. She had no trouble picking out the man who stopped her in the mall. "He was handsome with piercing blue eyes," she said. The photo she picked was Christopher Wilder's.

On April 1 the *Grand Junction Daily Sentinel* ran a front-page story on the missing girl. "You can't imagine what an awful feeling it is not to be able to do anything but sit here and wait," James Bonaventura was quoted as saying. "We're coping the best we can. Everyone has been just great, especially the police, who started looking into it instantly." The story mentioned the man posing as a photographer but did not say he had been identified as Christopher Wilder. Anyone with information was given a police number to call.

The FBI had quietly entered the case after Wilder's credit card receipts were traced to Grand Junction. They feared Sheryl had been kidnapped by the elusive Florida fugitive, but did not know which direction they had gone.

Wilder seemed to take no particular route, going one direction, doubling back, and heading another. There was no logic to his itinerary, no clue as to his next stop or final destination. He might have headed west on I-70 into Utah, doubled back to Denver and headed to Colorado Springs, or north to Wyoming.

The FBI had been able to follow Wilder by the charge cards he had stolen from his business partner, L. K. Kimbrell, which he used to purchase gas and motel rooms. Kimbrell had purposely not canceled the cards so the Bureau would be able to track the Florida fugitive.

The FBI learned that a man using Kimbrell's stolen cards bought a lunch at a roadside restaurant in Silverton, a town of less than a thousand located off State 550, about a hundred miles south of Grand Junction. A waitress told FBI agents that a man in his thirties, with thinning blonde hair and a beard, and a pretty blonde-haired woman in her twenties had eaten lunch on March 29.

The young woman approached another waitress and said she was Sheryl Bonaventura and that her uncle was Nick Bonaventura and used to live in Silverton. Sheryl said her uncle made doughnuts.

"The girl had a singsong voice, like she was talking baby talk," the waitress told the agents. "She said they were going to Durango to visit relatives before heading to Las Vegas, where she and another girl were going to be models."

As they talked, the woman's companion stepped up beside her. "I asked the girl if she wanted to sign the register," the waitress said. "The man gave her a look like, don't sign it, and she didn't."

The waitress was under the impression that Sheryl was enthused about the modeling opportunity. She also got the impression that Sheryl was nervous and giving her a lot of information, although the waitress didn't know why.

Photo lineups were shown to the waitress, who had no trouble picking out Christopher Wilder and Sheryl Bonaventura as the two who ate in the café.

The waitress said a young woman in her teens or

early twenties had also eaten with the couple and left the restaurant with them. She didn't know who the girl was and could describe her only as in her late teens or early twenties, about five foot, two inches tall and blonde. The description did not fit any of the women Wilder was suspected of kidnapping.

That evening a "Mr. and Mrs. L. K. Kimbrell" checked into a motel in Durango, Colorado, thirty-six miles south of Silverton. No one saw Wilder or the girls he ate lunch with go to the room, and no one saw them leave the following morning.

On April 4 the *Grand Junction Daily Sentinel* ran a story that reported Christopher Wilder was the chief suspect in the Sheryl Bonaventura disappearance and in the murder-abductions of six other women. The paper ran photos of the two under the headline "Sex Offender Linked to Grand Junction Case."

A reward fund was established for information about Sheryl that totaled more than $6,000. Crime Stoppers of Mesa County, Inc., had also offered a reward up to $1,000 for information, which could be made anonymously.

Sheryl's mother told reporters that she was furious to learn her daughter's suspected kidnapper was a past sex offender free on bond.

"I hope his lawyer never sleeps another night in his life," she said. "Just because Wilder has money, he's out."

By the time the story appeared, Wilder had fled to Nevada, to add another name to the "beauty queen killer" list.

Chapter Twelve

By all rights, seventeen-year-old Michelle Korfman never should have been an entrant in the *Seventeen* magazine cover model competition held Sunday, April 1, at the Meadows Mall in Las Vegas, Nevada.

Michelle had never entered a beauty contest before. And to be truthful, she was not all that interested in modeling. Still, she was intrigued. Could she do it? Would she place?

Physically, Michelle had no problem measuring up to the hundreds of other young hopefuls who had entered. At five feet, nine inches tall and a well-proportioned 130 pounds, she had the measurements to fill out a bathing suit or do justice to any clothing she wore. The pretty, dark-haired teenager was also photogenic. Her piercing blue eyes were set into a pretty, angular face that was bordered by deep curls of brown hair that cascaded down her back. Like model Brooke Shields, she combined the girlish innocence of a teenager with the classic beauty of a mature woman.

It was this girl-woman look that gave her an edge over the other contestants who had more experience. Besides, Michelle saw it as a challenge, and Michelle never shied away from a challenge.

"She came off as someone who would attack the world," a friend of hers once noted. "There were a lot of different things she wanted to be, but it was always something big."

Michelle was the second of three daughters born to Las Vegas casino executive Tony Korfman. The family had been raised in Las Vegas, but five years earlier Korfman decided to get out of the Las Vegas area and moved to Boulder City, a close-knit "green oasis" thirty miles south near Boulder Dam. He moved, he said, because Boulder City was a safe place to raise a family.

Michelle excelled in the small town environment. In high school she kept her grade average up, played on the school volleyball team, and was a member of the drill team. In addition, she pursued an interest in photography and piano, which she had played for thirteen years.

In November of her senior year, she showed an interest in politics and was chosen one of five area students to be flown to Washington, D.C., as part of a program offered by the Close-Up Foundation, which acquaints students with the machinations of government. When she returned, Michelle joked with her best friend, Tammy Cook, about a career in politics and becoming the first woman President. They both laughed, but Tammy was not about to bet against her.

Michelle planned to attend the University of Las Vegas during her freshman year of college. She had an interest in computers and was already taking a computer class there three days a week, and an English course at Clark County Community College. She intended to finish her undergraduate work at Pepperdine University in Malibu, California.

Her introduction to fashion modeling was nothing more than a fling. Although serious about competing, she was not particularly serious about pursuing modeling as a career. It was just something new to do.

Having made up her mind, Michelle asked her father for money so she might have professional pictures taken. The photographer she had in mind was Andrew Cattoir, a studio photographer at The Imagination Workshop in Boulder City, who had prepared portfolios for other aspiring models.

"She was very green," Cattoir recalls. "It was obvious she had never posed for a camera before." But once Michelle loosened up, Cattoir saw something else that was perhaps even more important than experience. Michelle was able to project personality onto film. "She had an attitude that came through," he said. "It was an attitude that said, 'Hey, I know what I'm doing.' It was an attitude that made you think she wasn't inexperienced, that she was confident and success oriented."

Michelle purchased two sets of photos from Cattoir, one to be used for the *Seventeen* competition, the other for the Mint Hotel, which each year hired a trophy girl for the Mint 400 off-road car race.

Cattoir shot two different styles. The first series showed Michelle in a pair of blue gym shorts and an abbreviated pink T-shirt with the words 'Grand Canyon' embossed on the front. Close-ups showed little expression on Michelle's face, a "frozen quality" perhaps attributable to her lack of experience. In the second series, for the Mint, Cattoir wanted her "to look a little more sophisticated" and had her pose with teased hair and wearing a shiny black top and a red jumpsuit. She was perched on a wooden stool in various hand-on-the-hip poses.

Cattoir was more impressed with the second set of photographs. She was more relaxed and her confidence seemed to leap off the finished print.

"She seemed to be a very trusting type of person, very outgoing," Cattoir recalls. "The word naive didn't apply. I did another girl for the contest and she was quite different. Just no confidence at all."

Michelle submitted the first set of photos to the *Seventeen* judges. They liked what they saw and selected her over hundreds of other contestants to be one of the fifteen finalists to pose for competition at the Meadows Mall on Sunday, April 1.

Normally someone—a family member, her boyfriend, or a friend—would have accompanied Michelle to the contest. But it was her first taste of modeling, and she was nervous.

"She specially asked that we not go to the mall,"

Rosario Gonzalez, 20, was last seen alive February 26, 1984. Her body has never been found.

Elizabeth Kenyon, 23, disappeared March 4, 1984; body never found.

Sheryl Bonaventura, 18, disappeared on March 29, from a shopping mall near her home in Grand Junction, Colorado. Her body was not found until after Wilder's terror spree had ended with a self-inflicted gunshot.

Dawnette Sue Wilt, 16. Abducted from a shopping mall in Gary, Indiana. She was stabbed and left for dead in Penn Yan, New York. Although badly wounded, she survived her three days of terror as a captive of Chris Wilder.

Beth Dodge, 33, was Wilder's last victim, found dead near Rochester, New York.

Michelle Korfman, 17, never returned from the beauty contest in which she was competing in Las Vegas. The two month search for her ended on June 15, when an unclaimed body in the Los Angeles County Morgue was identified as that of the missing teenager.

Terry Ferguson, 21, last seen alive in a Florida shopping mall. Her body was found six days later.

Terry Diane Walden, 24, didn't arrive to pick up her child from her day care center in Beaumont, Texas, on Friday, March 23. Her body was found in a canal three days later.

Suzanne Wendy Logan, 21, disappeared from the Penn Square Shopping Mall in Oklahoma City on March 25. She had been dead less than an hour when her body was found in a reservoir the next day.

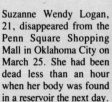

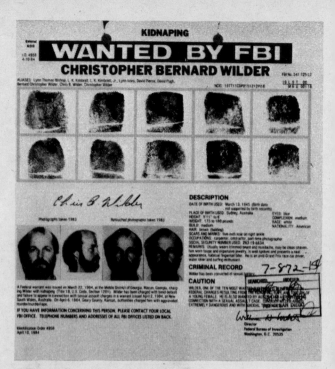

F.B.I. wanted poster for the object of one of their largest manhunts in the nearly seventy year history of the bureau.

her father recalls. "She didn't even tell her boyfriend about it."

Michelle arrived at the Meadows Mall in Las Vegas at noon, wearing a light-colored blouse, blue jeans, and white boots. She was directed to the dressing rooms at the Broadway Department by *Seventeen* officials, where she was told what to expect and was given the clothes she was supposed to model.

A crowd had already gathered for the highly publicized event, and by the time the contest got under way, the stage area was jammed. One of the photographers that afternoon was the mother of a contestant. As she jockeyed for position in the pushing and shoving crowd, the camera went off inadvertently.

When the roll was developed, a negative showed the back of a model from the waist down, her legs and laced shoes burned out by the flash.

Across the stage in the area reserved for fashion and news photographers, sat a man ogling the models. He wore white pants, a plaid shirt, and brown jacket, and sat with his hands clasped, one foot slightly behind his other leg and bright red purses just to his right.

Though he had shown a photographer's pass to get to the area, Christopher Wilder expressed no interest in taking pictures. The Pentax camera he had taken to shopping malls across the country was nowhere in sight. Instead, his full attention was directed at the young model in the light-colored miniskirt and carrying a bouquet of flowers.

*   *   *

Michelle had planned to return home for dinner after she finished with the contest. Dinner hour came and went, with Michelle's father anxiously waiting for his daughter's return. He wanted to talk to her about the contest, how it had gone, and, more importantly, how she felt about it.

He expected her around six. As the hour grew late, he became concerned. Michelle was never late for anything. She would not miss dinner unless something happened to her.

Shortly before midnight, Tony Korfman called the police to report his daughter missing.

In the investigation that followed, detectives repeatedly searched the Korfman house looking for clues.

In her room they found a Boulder City High School yearbook with pictures of Michelle posing with her volleyball team, and a "favorites" list, naming her favorite musical group (Rolling Stones, The Who), movie (*An Officer and a Gentleman*), best friend (Tammy Cook), and classes (drill team, American Literature). They also found a "priority" list in Michelle's clear, neat handwriting, reminding her to purchase a new dress for the May 5 senior prom.

They found nothing that suggested Michelle had decided to leave home, or where she might be.

Cities like Las Vegas receive perhaps more than their share of missing persons reports. But this one sent a thin wire of fear through the detectives assigned to investigate the case as well as residents who followed it in the newspapers and on the television news.

The Las Vegas Police Department was already investigating the murders of three women. They were all pretty, although separated in age by up to twenty-nine years, and all disappeared while minding their own business.

Lisa Traver was the first. A twelve-year-old seventh grader, she disappeared October 19, 1983, while walking home from school. Two teenage boys found her body twelve days later at the west end of Ann Road. She had been beaten to death.

Two months later, on December 30, Diane Rae Hanson, a twenty-two-year-old marketing and advertising major at North Texas State University, left her parents' home in Las Vegas to go jogging. She usually jogged two miles and returned to the house in twenty minutes. Later that night, her parents reported the attractive blonde coed missing.

A man picking up firewood found her nude body the next day at the west end of Spring Mountain Road. She had been raped and stabbed to death.

A forty-three-year-old suspected drug user who tried to outrun police on January 19 was questioned in her death but later dropped as a suspect.

The most recent and perhaps most perplexing of the three was the murder of Nancy Menke, the forty-one-year-old wife of an Air Force lieutenant colonel and mother of four. On March 20 she left work at the Fashion Show Mall and stopped to buy a pair of shoes at the Boulevard Mall on the way home. Junior high school students walking to school the next day found the woman's body in her car along Lamb Boulevard. The pretty, dark-haired housewife had been shot in the head and garroted with a nylon stocking that wrapped around her neck. She had also been sexually assaulted.

Exhaustive investigations were conducted, with as many as forty detectives assigned to a single case. Sex offenders were hauled in, hundreds of leads were checked out. By the end of March, police still did not have a suspect.

Though the cases appeared unrelated, police were not going to concede the point. Now, with the disappearance of the seventeen-year-old high school senior from the Meadows Mall, detectives wondered if a fourth file was going to be added to the others.

Michelle drove to the mall in the 1982 chocolate-brown Camaro, which her father bought her for maintaining a high grade average and staying out of trouble. The car had a personalized license plate that read "TOMISH" (To Michelle), and was fitted in a black frame reading "Daddy's Girl."

The car was not at the Meadows Mall, which police searched repeatedly. The investigation did turn up one witness who said she had spotted Michelle leaving the dressing area at the Broadway Department Store with a man.

He was described as in his forties, with light brown hair and beard, and wearing white slacks and a brown or dark-colored jacket.

Days later detectives would show the witness a photo lineup of known sex molesters who live in Las Vegas or were suspected of being in the area.

The woman had no trouble picking out Christopher Wilder as the person Michelle left the store with.

Michelle was not the only woman approached at the beauty contest Sunday afternoon. Eight women said they had been approached by a "photographer" who said he needed models for a magazine presentation he was putting together.

All turned him down.

Detectives also learned that a man matching Wilder's description and using the same con had talked several teenage girls into meeting him at Caesar's Palace for some picture taking. The girls arrived in front of the mammoth hotel located at the end of the Las Vegas Strip, but the photographer never showed.

An all-points bulletin was placed on Michelle's chocolate-brown Camaro and the burnt-orange Mercury Wilder had stolen from Terry Walden in Beaumont, Texas.

At 8:30 Monday morning, a guest at Caesar's Palace was walking toward his car parked in the rear lot when he spotted the chocolate-brown car parked in the rear lot. Having heard news reports about the girl's disappearance, the tourist called police.

Authorities found the doors locked and the trunk empty. A dried flower, apparently from the beauty contest, was still on the dashboard as police towed the locked car from the lot.

In the days that followed, FBI agents learned Wilder had arrived in Las Vegas on March 29, and spent the night at a downtown motel on Tenth and Fremont streets. He paid cash for the room and signed in under his own name. The motel was a clean if nondescript place frequented by small-time gamblers and vacationing couples on a budget. A few people recalled seeing someone like Wilder at the motel. He was alone, and no one recalled a young woman matching the description of Sheryl Bonaventura or the other young women whom Wilder was suspected of kidnapping.

The next day Wilder checked in at the Strip Motel not far from Caesar's Palace. Again he signed the register as Christopher Wilder and paid cash for the room.

Police technicians went over both rooms for physical evidence. They hoped they might find fingerprints to prove that one or more of his victims was with him and still alive. The rooms, however, had been rented out several times by the time the FBI was notified, and technicians were unable to raise usable prints.

The kidnapping of the young contestant from the *Seventeen* magazine contest was a big news story in Las Vegas. It was played on the front page of the daily newspapers and was the lead story on the TV news.

In the small community of Boulder City, it was more than a story: it was a personal tragedy that affected almost everyone.

"People who live here view Boulder City as a clean, green oasis away from the world," said Brian Fox, principal of the seven-hundred-student Boulder City High School. "What it really did is make the kids realize that these things happen out there. It really nailed people hard and it proved that 'out there' is here too. It brought the whole cruel world right to home base."

The Korfman family offered a $10,000 reward for Michelle's safe return and prosecution of the person responsible for her disappearance. Another victim of tragedy, Sol Sayegh, the owner of the Carpet Barn whose son was kidnapped seven years ago and never found, donated an additional $5,000. The Secret Witness program then added $1,000 for information on Wilder's whereabouts.

Persons with information were given telephone numbers for the FBI, the Metropolitan Police Department's missing persons detail, the Boulder City Police Department, and the Secret Witness program.

Calls poured in by the hundreds. Some fit the category of crank calls that police are used to getting in highly publicized cases. Others sent police officers racing through the city streets certain of an arrest.

Several students at Las Vegas High school told police they had spotted Wilder ogling girl students as they left the main school entrance and exit. By the time a squad arrived, the man had gone.

Police were also called to the Rancho High School in North Las Vegas where a man matching the sex slayer's description was also sighted. He too disappeared without a trace.

Others, meanwhile, told police they had spotted the elusive fugitive near Lake Tahoe on the California-Nevada border late Sunday, just a few hours after Michelle disappeared. A search was unable to confirm if the person was Wilder or someone who resembled him.

Police also received calls from young women who said they had been approached in shopping malls by a man who said he was a photographer. The suspect did not resemble Wilder, and police suspected that a "copycat" was at work, trying to cash in on Wilder's infamy.

Then, on Saturday night, police got a call from a madam at the Mustang Ranch, the legalized brothel east of Reno. One of her girls, the madam said, had noticed a customer who looked like Wilder, whose FBI wanted bulletin hung in the kitchen.

Was he still there? Yes, the madam said, but hurry.

Deputies from Storey and Washoe counties surrounded the brothel and arrested the man at the bar while he was sipping a beer.

The man protested, saying he was an electrical contractor from San Jose, California.

"The guy looked just like the guy on the wanted bulletin," said Captain Bill Tilton of Storey County. "Even had the same occupation. We figured we had Wilder."

Instead, they had an electricial contractor from San Jose. He was held until his fingerprints were checked against Wilder's, then released.

"I have no complaints about the way the police treated me," the contractor said. "They were just doing their job, even though I could see they were disappointed I wasn't the guy. That would have made their careers. The only thing that worries me is that someone else might make the same mistake."

Chapter Thirteen

As the search for Florida's most infamous fugitive spread across the state of Nevada, Christopher Wilder headed west across the wind-swept high desert toward Los Angeles.

On April 3, he arrived in the smog-shrouded town of Lomita, forty miles south of Los Angeles. California papers had not yet showed interest in the cross-country murder spree, and Wilder traveled here in relative obscurity.

That afternoon he spent $39 to sleep in a rundown room at the Proud Parrot Motel near the Torrance Municipal Airport. He signed in alone and used his business partner's credit card to pay for the room.

That evening the desk clerk heard someone banging on the soft drink machine outside the office and shouting obscenities.

"What's the problem?" the desk clerk asked.

"This goddamn machine wouldn't give me my soft drink," Wilder snarled, hitting the machine with a closed fist. Wilder was consumed with rage. His body shook as he hit the machine, and his eyes were glassy and bloodshot.

The clerk later told police he thought the man was drunk or crazy or maybe both. "Okay, okay, I'll give you your money back," the clerk said, "Just don't hurt the machine anymore."

Wilder checked out the following morning. He ate breakfast at a small coffee shop by the airport, and filled his gas tank at a Texaco gas station. That afternoon he parked at the Del Ammo shopping center to begin scouting his next victim.

At noon he spotted a pretty blonde-haired teenager walking into the Hickory Farm delicatessen. He followed her in and stood behind her while she made out an application for a summer job.

On the way out, he stopped her and asked if she would be interested in earning money as a model. Showing her a business card, he explained he was a photographer and that she would be perfect as a model for a billboard ad he was shooting. He said he would pay $100.

The teenager showed interest. Yes, she said, she could use the $100. When he asked her to accompany him to the beach to shoot a few test rolls, she agreed.

They drove along the scenic Pacific Coast Highway to a secluded beach near Santa Monica about ten minutes north of the teenager's home in Torrance.

Wilder shot a roll of film of the girl posing in the sand. But when the girl said she had to get home, Wilder became enraged. He whipped out a pistol, jammed the barrel into her mouth, and cocked the hammer.

"Your modeling days are over," he said.

He tied her up and drove 237 miles southeast to the small California town of El Centro, where he registered at the El Dorado motel.

Wilder no sooner checked in than he decided to leave. With his victim at his side, he left El Centro at five o'clock and headed east. He still drove the burnt-orange Cougar stolen from Texas, now fitted with a New Mexico license plate, swiped during his trip west.

That night he registered at the Motel 6 in Prescott, Arizona, a former silver-mining town turned retirement community a hundred miles north of Phoenix. The girl was forced into the room, tied to the bed, and sexually humiliated and tortured until Wilder finally fell asleep.

The next morning they left.

Sixteen-year-old Tina Marie Risico was missed almost immediately. She called her boyfriend on Wednesday morning, April 4, and said she was going to stop by the Del Ammo Mall after school and make out a job application at Hickory Farm.

Tina's parents learned she made it to the store at

11:45 A.M. When she didn't return to the house that night, they went to the police.

The detective who initially investigated the missing persons report learned the pretty blonde teenager was a troubled young woman with lots of problems.

Tina's parents divorced when she was two. Her father went to live in Santa Ana, California, where he landed a job as a telephone solicitor. Tina and her mother went on the welfare rolls.

"Life hasn't been easy for me or my daughter," Tina's mother said. "Tina has known the definition of starving. She's been hungry before."

Tina moved to Mendocino County north of San Francisco where her mother married a free-spirited Apache Indian, who subsequently died.

Then four years ago they returned to Southern California and moved into a small house in Torrance occupied by Tina's grandmother. It was a stormy living arrangement, with the grandmother and mother not always seeing eye to eye.

"She and I do not like each other in a lot of ways," the mother later told the *Los Angeles Times*.

According to friends, Tina grew up hard and fast—smoking pot in her early teens and talking about hard drugs like Quaaludes and LSD. She dropped out of two high schools and was finishing her education at Kurt T. Sherry High School, a continuation school.

Despite the turmoil in her life, Tina seemed on the verge of turning it around. Teachers said she was doing well in her studies, and she had landed a job at a Torrance restaurant that served low-calorie gourmet food. In March she talked of quitting her job at the restaurant and finding something else for the summer that paid better. She heard about the opening at Hickory Farm and went to apply.

Detectives questioned the manager at Hickory Farm, who remembered the young applicant with the china-blue eyes. He said she seemed efficient and friendly—just the sort of person they were looking for, and she had been hired for the summer.

Why, then, had she disappeared?

The manager told police about the man who followed Tina out of the store, describing him as in his late thirties, with a beard, and a camera strung around his neck.

"He said something about being a photographer," the manager said.

A few days later detectives showed him a photo lineup. "That's the one," the clerk said, pointing to Christopher Wilder.

Wilder by then had become something of a household name. Stories of the Florida fugitive had been aired on the local television news and published in the *Los Angeles Times*, the state's largest circulation daily. Overnight, he had become a celebrity.

Naturally, the Torrance police missing persons detail was swamped by callers who had seen the elusive killer.

"We had so many calls I can't begin to think how many," admitted Sergeant Rollo Green, who headed the missing persons detail.

Officers were pulled out of police specialty training schools to help the missing persons detail.

Wilder seemed to be everywhere: at shopping malls, cruising the freeways, hanging out at the beach.

A twenty-six-year-old graphic artist living in nearby Redondo Beach told police that she had been approached over the weekend by a man matching Wilder's description.

"He asked if I took pictures or did photography," the woman said. "I tried to ignore him."

The man then offered to let her take pictures of him and asked if she would like to go to dinner. As she walked away, the man just stood there and said, "Are you sure? Won't you change your mind? You never know, you might like me."

Another woman told detectives about a man driving a beat-up van who pulled up next to her car on Hawthorne Boulevard in Torrance and "just kept staring through the window. It gave me the creeps."

Some calls couldn't be checked out, like the woman who told police to meet her at a phone booth. "I am watching him right now," she said. "He's at a hot dog stand. He is having a hot dog right now!" When police arrived, the man was gone.

Ten or fifteen calls came from psychics. One suggested detectives look in a shopping mall in Riverside. Riverside police swept the area but found no sign of Wilder or Tina Risico.

Another psychic said the girl's body could be found in some bushes. The dispatcher asked if the psychic could be a bit more specific, since there were quite a few bushes in California alone.

"I just see bushes," the caller said, and hung up.

Still another told police that she saw Wilder and

his latest captive boarding a United Airlines flight for Taos, New Mexico. There are no flights to Taos, since the small art colony north of Santa Fe has no airport, but detectives checked other flights to other cities.

Wilder wasn't on board.

On the Friday following Tina's abduction, police were tipped off that Wilder was trying to buy a one-way ticket to Australia. It came from a traveler who saw the man at the travel-agency ticket counter and overheard him. The call went out over police scanners and was overheard by the news media. When Torrance detectives arrived, television cameras were already filming the bewildered traveler.

"What the hell is going on?" he said. Though he had an Australian accent and matched the fugitive's description, he was not Wilder. He was taken to the police station for his own safety and then released.

colony north of Santa Fe. He selected a modest if comfortable motel on the outskirts of town that featured a king-size bed and heavy, Spanish Colonial-style furnishings.

The following morning he immediately left town, his haste due perhaps to a story in the morning paper that announced Wilder had been placed on the FBI's Ten Most Wanted List. If becoming the 385th person to make the Bureau's hall of infamy wasn't bad enough, two days later he was treated to the shock of seeing himself give an interview on television.

His TV debut occurred almost by accident. An owner of a Florida video dating service had spotted a story about Wilder in the local paper. The name meant nothing to him, but when Wilder's picture was published after making the Ten Most Wanted List, the dating service owner called the FBI.

"The guy used our service," he told the Miami office. "I got him on videotape."

The tape was made in 1981, just months after Wilder was put on probation for the rape of the fifteen-year-old Tallahassee girl.

Relaxed and smiling occasionally, he told the video dating service interviewer, "I want to date. I want to meet and enjoy the company of a number of women. I have a need to meet and socialize on a more wider basis than I have been doing."

Wearing a beige sweater that revealed lots of chest hair, and a silver medallion around his neck, Wilder complained he had worked too hard and too long building his successful contracting business and wanted to play more. "This is a new change in myself hopefully," he said, looking pleased. "I am going to start getting out and away, specially from work."

Wilder was encouraged to describe his pastimes and interests. "Oh," he said, stroking his beard, "I have quite a few playthings at home. I like to drive sports cars, and I keep a couple of what you would call 'fantasy cars' at home."

Like many singles seeking a mate, Wilder was not comfortable with the bar scene.

"Bar-hopping is not, and never has been, one of my greater joys," he said. "Oh, I don't mind a social drink—I enjoy a social drink. And I like nice dinners out in the evening at some of the nicer places. But it has also reached a point where I can't go to Big Daddy's and feel comfortable. I'm a little bit out of that category."

"What are you looking for in a mate?" the interviewer asked.

Seated on the beige couch in front of a wood-paneled wall, Wilder said he wanted something more out of a woman than just a few good times.

"My objective is hopefully meeting the right person. Somebody with depth. Somebody that might have some background. Somebody that I can feel comfortable with. Quite frankly, I am seeking a long-term relationship that might one day become permanent. Right at this moment I am not seeking marriage, but someday I will."

The handsome bachelor told the young women who were to view the tape—women Wilder said should be no older than their early twenties—of his days growing up in Australia, being careful to leave out his arrest for gang rape and his electric shock treatment.

"Between the age of fourteen and twenty-four, I was heavy into surfing. That was my sole game in life. Arriving here in Florida and finding no surf, I went from one extreme to the other. I was completely non-work-oriented prior to coming here.

"Taking away that particular hobby, that particular facet of my life, I changed over completely from one extreme to the other.

"I get the urge now and again to go back to those places I lived in as a child," Wilder said, his voice a bit emotional. "I want to go back to Hawaii, go back to Sydney, particularly the east coast of Queensland where I spent a lot of my younger years."

The acquisition of the tape was, in the words of one Miami-based FBI agent, "a bonanza. It tells us a lot about his personality and about the man."

The interview showed no hint of the criminal mind, nothing that indicated the dark side of Wilder's personality which now totally consumed him.

What the tape did reveal was the personality of a consummate actor who could slip into any role in order to elude the massive manhunt that had been launched to find him.

That evening the FBI released copies of the tape to local television stations and networks.

"We are doing this so young girls can know what he looks like and what he sounds like," FBI agent Dennis Wrich said. "And God forbid, if he approaches you, don't go near the guy."

The release of the tape served not only the purpose

of warning potential victims, but also made Wilder's bearded face known to the millions who didn't read newspapers, or were not aware of him.

The decision to go public was effective because police departments across the country began receiving calls from persons who said they had seen Wilder. Television news departments hired behavorial psychologists to review the tape and reveal what it meant, while police officers told television viewers what to do if they were approached by someone like Wilder.

The tape generated public interest and nowhere was it greater than in the South Florida cities that Wilder had used as his personal playground.

Reporters and television news teams made pilgrimages to the shuttered and locked home on Mission Hill Road. Residents who had barely known Boynton Beach's infamous playboy found strangers knocking at the door asking what he was like.

"I guess we are famous now," harrumphed one home owner.

Everyone managed to come up with something.

"He was a bachelor, and we thought he had a lot of girlfriends," said George Mayhew, a Mission Hill resident who lived directly across the street from Wilder. "Many is the time when we looked up from the kitchen table at the sound of a car door slamming across the street to see yet another new face. We commented that they looked like, well, not models, but they brought a lot of clothes in shopping bags."

Another was impressed by the care and love Wilder showered on his three English setters, while Regina Bankowski remembered he "had a nice face, pretty blue eyes, and good skin. We thought he had some money."

Her husband, Ken, also thought Wilder was a rich guy, and recalled his one face-to-face encounter with Wilder as somewhat awkward. The mailman had left him a package intended for Wilder, and when he crossed the street to drop it off, Wilder met him at the front door in a bikini bathing suit, taking the package with a grunt. "It was from Frederick's of Hollywood," Bankowski explained, referring to the women's lingerie company. "I think he was embarrassed."

Perhaps the people who knew Chris Wilder best were the amateur race car drivers who competed with him at the Miami Grand Prix and other races.

"If I were to draw up a list of the five nicest guys I know, Christopher Wilder's name would be somewhere on that list," said Van McDonald, a Holmes City, Florida, race driver who had raced with Wilder for fifteen weekends a year for two years. "He was a super gentleman, generous to a fault. He's the exact opposite of what I've read about him. If it's all true, he's the biggest Jekyll and Hyde I've ever seen."

No one was surprised more by Wilder's notoriety than Vicki Smith, a pretty twenty-seven-year-old brunette from Fort Lauderdale. She raced cars with Chris Wilder, danced every Thursday night with him, and considered him one of her best friends. Vicki saw him as an old-fashioned gentleman, the type of guy who always opened the door and offered you his hand to help you out.

"A classic gentleman of a hundred years ago," she said. "The type of guy you bring home to your parents. You always had elegant times when you went out with Chris Wilder."

She at first didn't believe the FBI portrayal of Wilder as a warped psychopath who stalked shopping malls for eager young women he could lure with promises of modeling careers. That wasn't the Chris Wilder she knew.

Only later did she remember going to a shopping mall one day and bumping into Wilder, who was standing outside one of the department stores with a camera strapped around his neck. He seemed nervous and embarrassed to see her. She also remembered attending a fashion show with Wilder at which he knew the name of every model on the stage before it was announced.

"How he could function so normally for so long, I don't know," Vicki mused. "It is beyond my comprehension."

Two days after Wilder fled Florida, Palm Beach County deputies searched the canal behind his home for the bodies of the missing Beth Kenyon and Rosario Gonzalez. They found nothing of consequence in the canal, but inside the house they discovered the garage had been turned into a photographic studio equipped with colored backdrops, track lighting, makeup kits, and fans that gave models a windswept look.

The hidden studio led to speculation that Wilder might be into pornography, a rumor that gained credibility when an employee at the Boynton Beach K

Mart opened a package of photos Wilder had brought in for developing and found pornographic pictures of women and prepubescent children—many perhaps rendered compliant with the hypnotic drug that Wilder had admitted using in the 1980 rape case.

There was even a rumor that the Boynton Beach police were involved in the investigation of a white slavery ring being run by Wilder and a couple of his buddies.

But not every girl who made the trip back to the playboy pad on Mission Hill Road was asked to pose, or even was aware of the photo studio in the garage.

Twenty-one-year-old Ginnie Babcock met Wilder at the Banana Boat bar where she and her girlfriend had gone for a drink. Wilder sat down with them and started buying drinks. Tan and good-looking, he showed off his Rolex watch, the heavy gold chain around his neck, and the two flashy rings he said were diamond.

Ginnie didn't show any interest until he said he raced Porsches for excitement. That's my favorite car, she said. Let me take you for a spin, he insisted.

Ginnie thought he drove too fast, eighty miles an hour on the city streets, but she loved the reconditioned black Porsche, which smelled like new leather.

He took her back to the house, showed her the pool that overlooked the canal in the back, and crassly told her he had made millions in the construction business. Ginnie thought he was too hung up on things. Then, as he showed her the master bedroom, he tried to kiss her. Ginnie told him she wasn't interested, and he backed off. They went back to the bar where Wilder bought her another drink before telling her so long.

"He wasn't a bad guy," she said later, before the headlines indicated the opposite was true. "A little fresh, but nothing serious. And he did have the nice Porsche."

Another visitor to the Mission Hill Road house was Margaret Dawson, a thirty-two-year-old secretary with a Boynton Beach insurance firm. She met Wilder in the mid-1970s when "he had a fat beer belly and ran a topless bar in north Miami."

Off and on lovers over the years, she was aware of Wilder's playboy reputation, but knew nothing about the photo studio in the garage and saw no evidence he was mixed up in pornography or white slavery.

Margaret said only a few times did she suspect that there might be a dark side to her lover's personality.

Once, they were in the Jacuzzi together when a strange look came over Wilder's face. He jumped out of the Jacuzzi and told her to leave immediately.

"You have to get out of the water," he told her. "I can't tell you why, but you have to get out. I don't want to hurt you."

She got out of the water and went home. She didn't know what was wrong, but the look on his face had sent a chill through her. It was a Christopher Wilder she had never seen before.

Margaret saw the look just one other time when she woke up one night in her apartment in late 1983 and Wilder was standing at the foot of her bed, watching her. She had not expected him, and he had used his key to get inside.

His eyes had a wild look, she recalled. She had no idea how long he had been standing there. "Chris, what are you doing in my bedroom, what do you want?" she asked.

"I don't know," he said, snapping out of the trance. "I don't know why I'm here. I don't know how I got here."

In late 1982 Margaret had a daydream about her boyfriend that turned out to be real. In it, Chris was walking along the beach with a camera around his neck, a blonde teenage girl at his side.

When she told him about the dream, Wilder blanched and said he had been taking pictures of girls on the beach that morning.

He told the girls he was a professional photographer for magazines. It wasn't true, but he told them that so he could take their pictures and get near them. He didn't know why he took the pictures, but he had to. "It's like a sickness," he told Margaret. "I can't stop. It's something I have to do."

Chapter Fifteen

One person who thought he knew Christopher Wilder, only to conclude he didn't know him at all, was Tom Neighbors, an affable detective with the Palm Beach County Sheriff's Office.

Neighbors's casual friendship with the now-hunted fugitive stemmed from their mutual interest in sports car racing. When Wilder needed patches sewn onto his racing suit, he had Tom's wife do it.

Neighbors learned there was another side of his racing buddy when he read the FBI telex on March 21 naming Wilder as the suspect in the kidnapping-rape of the Tallahassee coed. Neighbors thought it was an odd coincidence the suspect had the same name as his friend and called the FBI for confirmation.

When he learned that the kidnap-rape suspect and

the sports car driver were one and the same, Neighbors put down the telephone receiver, stunned.

"I didn't think it could happen, at least not to me," he recalls. "We're cops, and we see things differently, judge people differently than your average citizen. But he had me fooled. I didn't see anything that made me suspect this other side of him."

Neighbors searched through the unsolved file to see if there were other sex crimes that fit Wilder's modus operandi. He found one that looked like a dead ringer. On June 15, 1983, a man with light brown hair and a beard approached two girls, ages ten and twelve, at the Boynton Beach City Park on Seacrest Boulevard and forced them into his car at gunpoint. He drove to a wooded area about twelve miles east of the city, where they were forced to perform oral sex. They were later returned to the park and told to tell no one what had happened.

Detective Neighbors located the girls and showed them a photograph lineup. Both identified Wilder as the man who had kidnapped and assaulted them. They also identified his Chevrolet El Camino as the car used in the abduction.

The Palm Beach detective also wondered if Wilder was involved in the deaths of two women whose remains were found on separate occasions in 1982 in an undeveloped, wooded area "very close" to eight acres of property owned by Wilder in Loxahatchee.

One of the women, whose skeletal remains were found in a shallow grave, had been dead for several years, while the other was dead for only a few months.

Neither was ever identified, but an examination of the bones and clothing found at the scenes indicated the victims were probably in their twenties or early thirties.

Wilder was also considered a suspect in other sexual assaults and murders in the state. Lee County Sheriff's officials determined Wilder was their best suspect in the case of two teens missing from a mall parking lot in 1981. Eighteen-year-old Mary Hare was later found stabbed to death, while seventeen-year-old Mary Optiz has not been found.

And detectives in Collier County, Florida, considered Wilder a suspect in the murder of Melody Marie Gay, a pretty nineteen-year-old clerk at a 7-Eleven store. She was working the graveyard shift at the store located on a desolate two-lane highway connecting the beach resort of Marco Island to the mainland in Collier County.

She was last seen alive at 4:30 in the morning of March 7 by a customer who strolled in for a pack of cigarettes. Three days later a fisherman found her nude body floating in a canal ten miles north of the store. She had been beatened and strangled.

Her death came just two days after Beth Kenyon disappeared. Police suspected Wilder because he made frequent trips to beach areas to search for victims.

The thirty-nine-year-old playboy was also a suspect in the disappearance of Colleen Orsborn, a fifteen-year-old student at Campbell Junior High School in Daytona Beach. One of six children from a tightly knit family, she was last seen asleep in her Buttler Boulevard home on March 15. The family told local authorities their daughter appeared happy and had never run away before. It was hoped the bubbly teenager had just left on impulse with a group of college kids or a friend. But as weeks passed, their spirits dampened.

Margaret Broomall, Colleen's older sister, organized a statewide search for the girl. She told police Colleen's brother and wife in Deland had just had a baby and that it was unlikely her sister would deliberately miss the happy event.

Authorities tended to agree. Just hours before she disappeared, Christopher Wilder checked into the Daytona Beach Howard Johnson Hotel. He was later seen strolling the beach with a camera around his neck, propositioning girls, and was placed near the Orsborn home the night she disappeared.

Meanwhile, police in Sydney, Australia, where Wilder was due to stand trial on kidnapping and sex charges, said they were investigating reports that Wilder had assaulted perhaps a dozen young women while he was visiting his family.

And in Miami, it was the same story. Detective Harvey Wasserman interviewed two dozen girls who had been sexually assaulted by Wilder. Metro Dade Detective Ray Nazario questioned forty.

"He degraded and humiliated so many people, especially young wide-eyed models," said Wasserman. "It was embarrassing for them to talk to us."

Wasserman found one young girl who had met Wilder at the Miami Grand Prix an hour before Rosario Gonzalez disappeared. She fit the type of woman that attracted Wilder—very young, very wholesome, clean-cut, in her midteens. Wilder wanted her to go with him to be photographed and gave her a business card with his name, address, and telephone number.

The girl was intrigued and about to go when her older sister showed up and stopped her. "I had a long talk with that girl," Wasserman said. "I told her if you believe in God, or go to church, that you go pray [because] your sister came along when she did."

Chapter Sixteen

A cold, hard rain swept across the grimy industrial city of Gary, Indiana, driving people back to the sweaters and bulky coats they had mothballed for the summer. But they had no sooner pulled out the coats than the cold front passed and the weather again was springlike, warm, and humid.

It was the early afternoon of April 10 when Dawnette Sue Wilt, a perky sixteen-year-old junior at Lake Central High School in Dyer, arrived at the Southlake Mall in nearby Merrillville, south of Gary, to submit an application for a summer job at Suzie's clothing shop.

While completing the form, a teenager stepped forward, introduced herself as Tina Marie Wilder, and said she worked at the shop. "You look like a good candidate for the job,'' Tina said and asked if Dawnette would wait outside the store while she fetched a manager.

The teenager named Tina returned a few minutes later with the ''manager,'' a handsome, balding man in his midthirties who had a deep tan and wore a gold chain and flashy rings.

Eyeing the pretty high school junior, he said he needed someone to model clothing at the shop and she seemed perfect for the job. Was she interested? He suggested they go to his car where he had some forms for her to sign.

In the parking lot, he pulled a gun from a briefcase and ordered Dawnette inside the Mercury Cougar. He bound her arms and legs and covered her eyes and lips with duct tape.

Tina drove while Wilder assaulted the girl in back.

That evening they stopped in the small town of Wauseon, near Toledo, Ohio, and rented a room at the Del Mar Motor Lodge.

Dawnette, her hands and legs tied, her mouth sealed with duct tape, was dragged into the room and treated to Wilder's perverse form of entertainment: electric shock and sexual sadism.

The following morning they crossed Ohio and Pennsylvania to New York, where they stopped at Niagara Falls. Wilder and Tina viewed the waters and took pictures, just like any other tourist couple, while Dawnette was kept hog-tied and gagged in the back seat.

That evening they checked into a room at the Exit 45 Motel, a modest, inexpensive place southeast of

Rochester. He signed the register Mr. and Mrs. L. K. Kimbrell of Boynton Beach, Florida, and paid with a credit card.

Wilder took Dawnette into the room while Tina lugged the suitcase. With the TV turned on, he plugged the electric shock device into the socket and taped the wire ends to Dawnette's body. Nobody at the hotel heard any screams as the teenager was raped and tortured for the second consecutive night. After he was through, he told both girls that he would kill them both if either tried to escape.

When Wilder woke the next morning, he turned on the television before taking one of the three or four showers he took daily.

Except for the female aerobics program, which he watched religiously, Wilder had little use for television and paid scant attention to the program that was on, *Good Morning America*, or its toothy host, David Hartman.

This show was different from most. A featured guest was Tina Marie Risico's mother, who looked straight into the camera and pleaded with Wilder to spare the life of her daughter.

Wilder started screaming. "We are getting the hell out of here," he growled, packing his few possessions and ordering his two captives to the car. Duct tape was slapped across Dawnette's mouth, her hands and feet tied, and she was again shoved into the back seat.

Wilder stayed clear of the New York State Thruway, taking back roads to Penn Yan, a tiny town set in the heavily wooded Finger Lakes region fifty miles south of Rochester. He pulled onto a dirt road, untied Dawnette's hands and legs, and pushed her into the woods. He had promised to let her go if she did what he wanted and did not try to escape. But that was one promise he had no intention of keeping. With her eyes still blindfolded by duct tape, she was forced down to her knees and told to sit still. Wilder retied her arms. With her helpless, he tried to suffocate her by pinching her nostrils shut.

When she pulled her head free, he yanked out the fillet knife he had used on the other women and plunged the long thin blade once into her chest and twice into her back. Dawnette crumpled to the ground, blood weeping from the savage wounds.

Satisfied she was dead or dying, he turned away and walked the three hundred yards back to the car, cleaning the blood off the knife blade with a handful of leaves he pulled from a tree.

Back in the car, he made a U-turn and retraced the route he had taken toward Rochester. Within two hours he was in the small town of Victor, looking for another shopping mall.

Dawnette's mother, Cheryle, spent three anxious days worrying about her sixteen-year-old daughter.

She had reported her daughter missing to Lake County, Indiana, police at seven o'clock Tuesday evening, three hours after Dawnette was supposed to have returned home from her interview at Southlake Mall.

Employees at the dress shop told detectives the pretty brunette high school junior had not shown up at the dress shop for the interview. Dawnette's 1977 Chevrolet Malibu was later recovered, but provided no clues as to the girl's whereabouts.

Friends of the missing girl said Dawnette had no reason to leave home. She was a popular girl at school, they insisted, and had high hopes of landing the job at the dress shop.

The interview had meant so much to her that she had planned to borrow an outfit from her girlfriend Diane Landorf, but instead wore one her mother had purchased for her just for the interview.

Dawnette's parents were divorced and her father lived in Indianapolis. The father, however, said the girl was not with him, and he had no idea where she might have gone.

The anxious parents did not learn the fate of their daughter until a New York State Policeman called on Friday afternoon.

Dawnette was in the Soldiers and Sailors Hospital in Penn Yan, New York. Amazingly, she was still alive.

One of the three knife wounds had come close to hitting her heart, but the spunky teenager had refused to die. Tied and gagged with tape, she had played dead until Wilder had left and she could try to summon help. The blood that streamed from her wounds made her hands slippery enough to pull free from the ropes. She tore the tape from her mouth and walked back to the dirt road. Realizing she was walking the wrong way, she turned around and headed back down the middle of the road. Using her shirt to staunch the flow of blood from her chest wound, she spotted a car making a turn in the road.

Tractor serviceman Charles Larson had gotten lost on the road and was turning around when he spotted the girl, the front of her clothing covered with blood, coming toward him.

"Please take me to a hospital," Dawnette asked.

The first one that came to mind was the Soldiers and Sailors Hospital. Larson put his foot to the floor and got there as fast as he could.

Doctors treated the young girl for severe trauma and loss of blood. After her condition was stabilized, she told detectives from the Yates County Sheriff's Office and the FBI office in Buffalo about the two days of terror at the hands of Christopher Wilder.

She said Wilder had been greatly upset by the appearance of Tina's mother on *Good Morning America*, and vowed that he would not be taken alive. For much of the time, she was blindfolded and hog-tied and didn't know where she was or where she was going, although her abductor had talked about heading into the Northeast and possibly crossing into Canada.

Information provided by the girl was broadcast through the Northeast. Police still held out hope that they would be able to rescue Tina Marie Risico and capture Wilder and make him tell where the other missing women were.

It came as something of a surprise to learn that Wilder was still driving the Mercury Cougar he stole from Terry Walden in Beaumont, Texas. The car had been on police hot sheets from coast to coast, and yet he had managed to elude capture.

Wilder had been lucky on his six-week odyssey across the country. But lady luck, once his friend, was about to turn on him.

Leaving Dawnette for dead off the rutted dirt road near Penn Yan, he retraced his route over country roads to Rochester. At noon he pulled off into Eastview Mall near Victor, New York, to look for a new getaway car. He found one to his liking, a 1982 gold Pontiac Trans-Am. It was driven by thirty-three-year-old Beth Dodge, a pretty Sunday school teacher, who was on her way to lunch.

Beth didn't keep her appointment. As she stepped from her car, a dark-haired teenage girl stopped her and asked her to come over to her car for a minute. When Beth was close to the Mercury Cougar, Wilder pulled the .357 Magnum and pushed Beth inside. Tossing the car keys to the Pontiac Trans-Am to Tina, he ordered her to follow him. She did.

Wilder headed the car away from the mall, then turned down a back road that led to a gravel pit. Pulling her from the car, he marched the terrified woman toward the pit, then pushed her to the ground. With no hesitation he shot her once between the shoulder blades, killing her almost instantly.

In all likelihood, Beth Dodge did not know why she had been abducted or who her abductor was.

"Why did Mommy have to die?" Beth's daughter Stephanie later asked. Neither her father nor anyone else was able to provide the answer. "There was no torture, no tape, no cord," said Captain Gerald Willower of the New York State Police. "Beth was just in the wrong place at the wrong time."

Her body was found later that afternoon. Investigators traced her movements to the shopping mall, where she had planned to meet friends for lunch.

When the Mercury Cougar Wilder had driven across the country was found abandoned near where her body was found, Beth's name was added to the "beauty queen" list and an all-points bulletin was put out for the missing gold Pontiac.

The attack on the Indiana teenager and the murder of the New York Sunday school teacher, both occurring within hours of each other, made Christopher Wilder the target of the largest police manhunt in recent memory.

Every man who wore a badge in the Northeast knew the description of the FBI's most wanted criminal and his teenage companion, and had memorized a description of his getaway car and its license plate. Evening newspapers carried stories of the latest murder, and TV news stations aired Wilder's video dating service tape, which had been so graciously supplied by the FBI.

But despite a manhunt the FBI termed the largest in history, Wilder managed to elude capture. No one spotted him on the New York State Thruway as he headed for Massachusetts. Nor did they spot him maneuvering through the treacherous Boston traffic heading for Logan International Airport.

No one would spot him until the following Friday morning at 9:15, when he drove north out of Boston on Route 128. Near suburban Beverly, Massachusetts, he spotted a nineteen-year-old woman standing beside her car, which had broken down.

Pulling in front of her car, Wilder stepped out to look over the problem, then asked if she needed a lift to a gas station.

The teenager said she did and said she knew of a gas station about a mile up the road. When they passed the station, she asked him to stop. Wilder pulled his Magnum and told her to shut up or die.

The woman shut up. But when they slowed for a traffic exit, the young woman pushed the door open and rolled out on the road shoulder. Wilder sped off into traffic as the girl ran for help.

Chapter Seventeen

The teenage girl stepped off the plane into the bright California sunlight and headed through the bewildering maze of corridors of Los Angeles International Airport, still clutching her one-way ticket stub from Boston.

For most of the other passengers, Delta Airlines Flight 933 from Logan International Airport to Los Angeles was just another long flight to the Coast with the usual problems of airline food and jet lag to contend with. For the blonde-haired sixteen-year-old who made her way through the terminal, it was likely the most memorable flight she would ever take. Having been threatened with death continually for the past nine days, she was certain she would not live to see the massive jet lumber down the Boston runway.

149

Only after the jet had climbed into the air and the no-smoking light blinked off, did she, for the first time, feel free. Only then did she realize that, unlike the others, she would live.

Walking out to the front of the airport, where cars darted for the curb to pick up passengers, she motioned for a cab. Taxis were no problem at this early hour, and a battered yellow cab with a tired-looking driver at the wheel pulled up.

"Where to?" he asked, noticing with regret that she did not have luggage, which meant she probably was not going very far.

She could have given the address to her home in Torrance, or the Torrance Police Department, where one way or another she would eventually have to go. But she didn't want to go home or to the police, at least not yet.

Thinking for an instant, she replied, "Hermosa Beach."

The lingerie shop with the coy name The Tushery, was open for business when she walked in at 11:45 A.M. and asked the assistant manager, Michelle Crone, if she could look at some "teddies"—lacy, one-piece undergarments.

The eighteen-year-old assistant manager took her to the front of the store where they hung on a long chrome rack. After looking through the selection, she asked Michelle if she had heard about the girl who had been kidnapped in Torrance.

Michelle said she had, that it was impossible to pick up a newspaper or turn on the television without another story about Tina Risico. It was a big story; everybody was talking about it.

"Well, that's me," Tina said. "I'm the one they're looking for."

Michelle was joined by Amy Clement, a sales clerk. Tina told them about being kidnapped at the Del Ammo Mall and being forced to drive across country.

It was the wildest story they had ever heard, but they didn't doubt for a moment that she was telling the truth.

"He kept telling me he was going to kill me unless I cooperated," Tina said in a calm, matter-of-fact voice. "He did these things to me, sexual things. He took this electrical thing and stuck it to my body."

The two store employees noticed purplish marks on Tina's chest, apparently left from the electric-shock instrument.

They also noticed Tina's hair. It had been cut short and badly styled by someone who obviously didn't know anything about cutting hair.

The man made her do it, Tina said. He wanted her to look like the girl from the movie *Flashdance*. He wanted all his girls to look like her.

"I don't want to call home yet," she told the clerk. "I want to think about it. I'm really confused. I needed to do some shopping and have some time alone because I figure I won't be alone much for a while."

Tina selected several garments and had the clerk ring them up. The total came to $104.50. She paid the bill from a large wad of bills in her purse, then went outside to catch a cab.

She had the cabbie go by her boyfriend's house. He wasn't there, and eventually two friends saw her and drove her to the Torrance Police Department.

Police are used to people coming to the station and telling odd stories. Police officer Emilio Paerels did not believe this was one of those reportings when the teenager walked into the station at 1:08 P.M. and identified herself as Tina Marie Risico.

His first reaction was that she appeared to be in a healthy condition. She didn't appear traumatized or physically hurt. There were a couple of bruises and her hair was cut oddly, but that was it.

Tina didn't know why her life had been spared. Wilder had threatened to kill her repeatedly since she was abducted. Then, after switching cars in New York he told her, "I don't want you to be with me when I die," and drove her to Logan Airport.

Tina said she believed that she was going to die anyway, no matter what Wilder told her. "I thought he was going to shoot me when I boarded the plane," she told detectives. "I almost collapsed when I made it inside."

After a three-hour interview, the pretty teenager was whisked past news reporters and cameramen who had formed a crowd outside the police station, and was taken to the Los Angeles County Harbor—UCLA Medical Center, where she was examined by Dr. Ronald Summit, a psychiatrist specializing in treating trauma cases.

He found the sixteen-year-old had been "subjected

broken into a home on Titus Hill and stolen a tool box and video cassette recorder. Someone else, or maybe the same person, had also swiped a white Pontiac from in front of the Cedar Lounge. The next day it was found parked in front of the IGA store with a $5 bill stuffed in the ashtray—a way of saying thanks for the car, and here's some gas money, police figured.

Even the big event of the week, the robbery of the Farmers and Traders Bank, had a folksy, small-town ring to it. At ten o'clock a man described as very tall approached teller June Hibbard and demanded the $300 in bills she was counting. June told him no— "After all, you don't go around just handing money out, right?"—and he grabbed the money and dashed for the door. The door was locked and wouldn't open. A customer walking into the bank noticed his distress and suggested he try the other door. The robber thanked him as he fled into the street.

He got as far as the Shrine of Our Lady of Grace, ten miles outside of town before he was forced to pull off the road by two police cruisers and was arrested.

It wasn't much, as bank robberies go, but it was the big news story in Colebrook, which had experienced only one other bank robbery in its 150-year history. And it was the topic of conversation when plainclothes State Police officers Leo "Chuck" Jellison and Wayne Fortier left the Speedy Chef restaurant for their unmarked green station wagon.

Jellison, a 6 foot, 4 inch, 250-pound veteran trooper, was a familiar sight in the small towns that comprise

New Hampshire's northern tip. He was taking Fortier, the new man on the job, around to meet local police officials and give him some pointers. For lunch that day they had been joined by Colebrook Police Chief Wayne Cross and State Trooper Howard Weber.

As they headed back to the police station, Fortier looked out the window and noticed a gold Pontiac Trans-Am parked in front of the gas pumps at Vic's station. Fortier remembered a television news report that morning of a woman being shot in Upstate New York and her car, a gold Trans-Am, being stolen. The suspect was some guy from Florida named Christopher Wilder.

"That looks like the car that Wilder guy is supposed to be driving," Fortier told his partner as they passed the station.

The police chief and the state trooper were dropped off at the police station, but on the way back Jellison slowed down by the gas station and took a look. Jellison noted the Trans-Am was fitted with a Massachusetts license plate, but the color and year matched the description of the one wanted by the FBI.

Jellison noticed something else too. The driver of the Pontiac, who stood talking to Wayne Delong, resembled photos on the wanted bulletin that the FBI had sent out. The Wilder guy had a beard, while this man was clean shaven, but the state trooper saw that the skin was white along the jaw and chin as if the man had recently shaved off a beard. The guy also had a deep tan—unusual for someone from the New England area this time of year.

"Let's go have a look," Jellison said, pulling the

unmarked green station wagon between the Pontiac and the gas station window.

The driver was walking back to his car when Jellison stepped up to him and said, "Excuse me, I'd like a word with you."

Wilder turned toward the trooper, the smile gone from his face. Jellison was dressed in plainclothes, but Wilder had no trouble making him out as a cop.

Wilder dashed for the car. The passenger door was locked, and he ran around to the driver's side and dove across the seat, grabbing for the .357 Magnum.

It happened so fast that Jellison didn't have time to draw his weapon.

Jellison could see that the man's hands, pulling away from the flopped-open glove compartment door, held something bright and shiny—a handgun.

An idea flashed through Jellison's mind: the man is going to kill me.

Faced with a man turning toward him with a gun in an enclosed place, Jellison did the only thing he could—threw himself inside the car and on top of the gunman. He gripped the struggling man beneath him in a massive bear hug, his sole intention being to keep the man's arms inside his own, so he could not turn the gun barrel and shoot him. But the gun barrel was moving, or Jellison thought it was. And with the brute strength that is born from fear, he pulled his arms in harder. "I am not going to let him shoot me," Jellison thought.

Then the inside of the car exploded, and Jellison felt a searing pain under his right rib. The explosion was followed immediately by another as Wilder stiffened, then went slack. Jellison released his grip and staggered backward.

Seventy-four-year-old Wilbur Grey was at the station, as he was every afternoon, to gab with his friends. He saw the motorist walk back to his car and the two detectives start chasing him.

"They was a scuffling inside and the next thing I know there were two loud pops. I expected to see bullets flying in here, so I got out of the way," Grey remarked.

Grey had no sooner ducked than there was another shot and he saw Jellison stagger over to his station wagon. While Detective Fortier ran around the car and covered the suspect's lifeless form, Jellison used his radio to clear all channels and call for help.

Reverend Joe Eastman had been coming out the door of the Independence Electronics shop when he noticed the two lawmen running around the car at Vic's gas station.

"I had gone to town in the afternoon to take my wife to the hairdresser's. I had some time to kill while she was in there, so I went over to Larry Rappaport's shop, you know, right across the street from the *Sentinel*. I had just stepped back out of the store when I heard this shot.

"There were these two men struggling over there at the station. The two men I could see the most of were the detectives. One of them got out of the car nearest the pumps, kind of staggering, right after I heard that sort of muffled shot. His partner was out of his car with his gun out, hollering his head off. It sounded like, 'Hold that car, hold that car, hold it.' He was really yelling at the top of his lungs.

"The detective went over and got into his own car, and he was sort of in there leaning. There was so much yelling, so much confusion, I thought it was another holdup."

A breathless Reverend Eastman arrived at the station to report the shooting just as Chief Cross and State Trooper Howie Weber were coming out of the door. They had learned of the shooting from a phone call.

"We ran right up the street," the chief recalls. "Howie grabbed his shotgun. I was the first one there. I could see Detective Fortier waving his arms and Chuck Jellison behind the wheel with his hand over his chest. I could see the blood.

"He said, 'I've been shot—get me some help now, Wayne.' And then I think he looked at the guy on the front seat and said, 'I think he's dead.'

"My sergeant, Ronald Martin, was up at Brooks Chevrolet with the cruiser. I called him to get right down, then go to the hospital to see if he could help get an ambulance and a medic here. They got here in a real hurry. I told one of the medics, 'Forget the guy in the car, he's dead. Take care of the guy in the cruiser.' Eric Stohl showed up to help Jellison until the ambulance arrived. So did Marybeth Weber, Howie's wife. She was walking down the sidewalk when it all happened. We reassured her that Howie was all right, and then she hustled over to help Chuck."

A crowd had gathered in front of the car parked at

the gas station pumps. They had been drawn to the staccato sounds of gunfire but were not yet aware of what had happened or of the identity of the victim.

Terry Rosi, the photographer for the *Sentinel*, had just come back from a photo assignment when he heard the shots from across the street. Grabbing his camera, he ran over to the station in time to see the police chief and state troopers attending to Chuck Jellison.

"Fella there's been shot," a bystander told Rosi, who began snapping pictures. Like others in Colebrook, he did not know that the man lying facedown on the front seat with his cowboy boots sticking out the door was one of the FBI's ten most wanted criminals.

Rosi was joined by another *Sentinel* photographer, sixteen-year-old Ward Thompson, as well as by Cameron Howard, the owner of Colebrook's only other restaurant, Howard's.

Howard, twenty-nine, was busy washing dishes at the restaurant when he got a call that there had been a weird shootout at Vic's gas station. A home-movie buff, Howard grabbed his Atachi home-movie setup and ran down to the station to videotape the scene. After learning the dead man might be that "maniac killer from Florida," he called the ABC affiliate in Maine and told them what he had. "They put me through to New York immediately. The people in New York told me they'd have a helicopter in Colebrook in forty-five minutes and sure enough they did."

The shooting of Christopher Wilder was the day's top news story in the country, and dozens of reporters and cameramen from the nation's media descended upon the isolated logging town, just a step behind investigators with the State Police, the State Attorney General's Office, and the FBI.

As they arrived, Chuck Jellison was being treated for a single gunshot wound to the chest at Upper Connecticut Valley Hospital. The angry slug that had killed Christopher Wilder had ripped through Jellison's chest, bruised one of his lungs, and finally lodged on top of his liver. The surgeon who removed the slug, Dr. Tom Cashero, said it missed killing him by an inch.

Despite his close brush with death, the trooper was able to get up and walk in the hospital the following day. He was eager to get back to work, but was told that it might take weeks of recuperation before he could put on a uniform.

Christopher Wilder's body, meanwhile, was taken by ambulance to Weeks Memorial Hospital in Lancaster, New Hampshire, where the autopsy was performed by pathologist Dr. Robert Christie. Both shots from the .357 Magnum pistol had hit Wilder square in the chest, the first penetrating the heart, then passing through the back and wounding Jellison. The first shot had caused massive blood loss while the second had slammed directly into the heart, causing, in the pathologist's words, "cardiac obliteration." Wilder's heart had literally exploded.

The time of death was put at 1:43 P.M. on Friday the 13th, forty-seven days after Rosario Gonzalez, the first of his thirteen suspected victims, had disappeared in Miami.

Chapter Nineteen

For the millions who followed the story of the "Beauty Queen Killer," the bloody shootout in the obscure New Hampshire town came as a shocking, if not welcome conclusion to a bloody real-life drama that had gone on far too long. Wilder was dead; he wasn't going to hurt anyone anymore.

But for the families of the girls who were still missing and the detectives who still had cases to solve, Wilder's death was yet another frustration in a case that was full of them.

Casino executive Tony Korfman had been conducting searches for his daughter Michelle since her disappearance from the *Seventeen* beauty contest in Las Vegas, Nevada, on April 1.

One search had led him to canyons in Floyd Lamb

State Park outside Boulder City after a psychic said she saw a body lying near some water. A few days later two hundred Boulder City residents, including elementary, junior, and senior high school students, combed through the ashes of the Sunrise Mountain area near Las Vegas.

"Mathematically, it's an extremely long shot that she's still alive," Korfman admitted. "But when you're a parent, you're always hoping for that long shot."

Korfman arranged for the filming of an interview with Wilder's brother Steven, in which the Florida fugitive was asked to tell the Korfman family what he had done with Michelle. The interview was scheduled to run on the evening of Friday the 13th, then scrapped after the announcement of Wilder's death.

"It's a shame he had to enjoy such a quick death. It's something I didn't wish him to enjoy," Korfman admitted. "But we still have to find Michelle. We have got to find her and put it to rest and get on with the rest of our lives. This has been a nightmare. I am forty-one and I don't think I have enough years left to get over this."

Similar searches were conducted in Colorado for the body of Sheryl Bonaventura, the nineteen-year-old aspiring model who was kidnapped from the Mesa Mall in Grand Junction. Since her disappearance, parties of as many as three hundred people in airplanes, four-wheel-drive vehicles, in boats and on horseback had helped the Bonaventuras seek their daughter in remote areas between Grand Junction and Las Vegas.

The search had been aimed at highways, side roads, drainage ditches, and anything that might be attractive to someone trying to hide a body.

Jim Bonaventura had been laid off his superintendent's job with Coseka Resources before the disappearance of his daughter, and had been offered a job by Leed Oil, a Texas company. He had not yet accepted the job. But when the company learned of Sheryl's disappearance, he was told, "You are on the payroll whether you take the job or not."

The income gave him time to look for his daughter. But after weeks of twelve- to fourteen-hour days of searching, he had not found a trace.

"I'm glad they got him and glad he's dead," Jim Bonaventura said. "I just wish he'd lived awhile and told where our daughter is and the rest of those girls."

His wife, Sandy, shared similar sentiments. "I first wanted something like all of the mothers of the victims to come together to get him. Now I feel it is just a shame that we couldn't have gotten a chance to find out how many girls he injured and who they were."

The family vowed to continue looking for Sheryl until they find her.

In Beaumont, Texas, Jack Graham greeted the news of Wilder's bloody demise with a sigh of relief—mostly relief that he wouldn't go to jail for killing the man who took the life of his daughter, Terry Walden.

"It was the best for him. And probably the best for me. He probably kept me from going to the penitentiary,'' Graham admitted. ''What I had planned for him wasn't any good. I would have found him and he would have ended up in the same canal where they found Terry's body.''

Dressed in bib coveralls and a white T-shirt, and standing in front of the clapboard home where his daughter was raised, Graham said he wasn't going to ''let the snake slide. He took the easy way out. That snake wasn't going to plead insanity and get off. You can write this off that I'm just spouting off, but that's wrong. Ask anyone who knows me. I had everything planned. I was prepared a week ago. The scope was on my rifle. I've got a quarter of a million dollars, and I would have spent every cent, even time in the pen, to get him.''

Terry's husband, John, believed his father-in-law. ''I'm afraid that if Jack had found Wilder he would have done something that would have hurt himself.''

As for his own feelings about Wilder, John reflected: ''Every time I heard someone else was killed by that maniac, it hurt me as bad as when they found Terry. I'm glad he can't hurt anyone else anymore, but I'm sick he took the coward's way out. I wanted him to answer questions we didn't have answers for.''

Jack Duchan, stepfather of twenty-year-old Suzanne Wendy Logan, was bitter that ''Wilder missed the electric chair. He got out of frying. At least that was my immediate reaction. But in retrospect, we have been pleased to be spared the grisly details of a trial.''

Duchan was still unhappy in the way police in

Oklahoma investigated his daughter's disappearance. "They should have done more. But they gave me the impression that they weren't really interested."

Don Ferguson, captain of the Indian Harbour Police Department and stepfather of twenty-one-year-old aspiring model Terry, was not unhappy it ended the way it did. "I was extremely pleased that they killed him. With our judicial system today, I wasn't looking forward to his being caught alive and watching him on TV, smiling and grinning and enjoying life while he got all the notoriety and publicity. The only bad feelings I have are for the parents of those who will never know, those whose girls are still missing. He was the only one who had the answers, and they will go through living hell forever."

Ferguson continued his practice of stopping for young hitchhikers whenever he spots them. "These girls don't understand what's going on today. This mass-murderer type of thing is becoming an epidemic. All you have to do is look at TV—every night they're picking up these crazies."

The sympathetic police captain might have been speaking directly to Bill and Delores Kenyon, whose efforts to find their daughter Beth had forced Wilder into the open.

"We had questions we wanted to ask Wilder," Kenyon admitted. "Now I don't know how myself or any of the other families are going to find the girls. You can't imagine what this has been like for us. I've never experienced anything like this in my life.

Any illness or death in the family was very sudden, but this has been a long, drawn-out thing. I pray it isn't going to be drawn out any longer.

"I wanted him caught alive. I would have spent my whole life waiting for them to pull the switch of the electric chair. But I wanted him alive because we wanted to know where Beth is."

The body of Christopher Wilder remained at the Newman Funeral Home in Colebrook, New Hampshire, three days until it was claimed by his brother Steven, who asked that it be flown to Florida for burial. Before it was removed, FBI technicians took additional footprints and fingerprints and hair samples and conducted other tests that they hoped might prove useful in their investigation.

On Tuesday afternoon, April 17, the body was put in a coffin and taken by hearse to Portland, Maine, where it was put on a Delta jet for West Palm Beach.

A brief funeral service was conducted the following afternoon at the Scobee-Combs Funeral Home in Boynton Beach. Wilder's body was dressed in a light gray suit. His body rested in an open oak casket during the brief service in a green-draped parlor, one of the home's smaller rooms. Only a dozen people attended the thirty-minute service, described by the funeral home spokesman as "a very ordinary Catholic service, with a priest brought in from Boca Raton. The family made the arrangements."

Amid those attending, amid tight security, was Wilder's brother Steven, and L. K. Kimbrell, Wilder's former business partner.

"It's hard for a friend to grieve for a friend that's done such terrible things," Kimbrell said. "There's a part of your mind that has to make sure he's gone and part of the nightmare is over. How else are you going to know unless you attend the funeral?"

Afterward, the body was cremated and the ashes given to the family for disposal—except for Wilder's brain, which had been removed during the autopsy and was being kept in a glass jar of formaldehyde in the office of Dr. Robert Christie, chief pathologist at Memorial Hospital in Lancaster, New Hampshire. The brain, along with portions of the other body organs, had been removed in order to perform the autopsy. "Routine stuff," is how Christie explained it.

On the 19th of April Christie got a strange call from a man identifying himself as a staff member of the psychiatric department of Harvard University Medical School. The caller asked if Christie still had the brain, and when the pathologist confirmed that it was still in his possession the caller asked if he could have it. He said he wanted to see if there were any physical abnormalities that might have triggered Wilder's violent behavior.

Christie told him he had already examined the brain and found it had no lesions or defects. It was quite a healthy-looking organ, weighing a bit over three pounds, approximately right for a man of Wilder's age and size.

The caller was insistent; he wanted the brain for

research—maybe Christie had missed something. Was it all right?

The pathologist informed the caller to make out a formal request on stationery with the Harvard University letterhead and he would submit it to the State Attorney General. If the request was okayed, then maybe he could.

The caller hung up. He never called back and never sent the letter. Christie later called Harvard Medical School and asked if someone in the psychiatric department had made the request. No one had; at least no one would admit to it. A spokeswoman said such a request was highly unlikely; she wasn't sure that Harvard would even make such a request.

"I don't know if it was legitimate or someone trying to cause excitement," Christie admitted. "We have had a lot of requests for body parts of this man. The FBI wanted his hands, and someone out in Kansas wanted his jaw—I guess because he might have bitten one of his victims. I am really amazed by the attention he has drawn. I am sixty years old and I've done a lot of autopsies, but I have never been involved in one that's created this much commotion."

Chapter Twenty

"Wilder wasn't much different than a lot of fellows I see every day."
—*Probation Officer Kim LaLonde*

During his twenty-six-day odyssey across the nation, Christopher Wilder had been described so often as a millionaire playboy that most people assumed he was. But after the shootout in Colebrook, New Hampshire, a rumor spread that his millionaire status was as fake as the zircon "diamond" rings he flashed at the young women in the Banana Boat bar.

Estimates of the estate only confused the issue. One placed it as high as $1.8 million, another put it at a bit less than $1 million. But even the low figure was misleading, because the sales of properties Wilder had accumulated would go for considerably less than what they were appraised at.

Richard Herold, a Palm Beach attorney named as estate executor, figured that "from a liquid standpoint, the estate will be closer to five hundred thousand dollars."

The inventory included properties Wilder had purchased in West Palm Beach and in Brevard and Dade counties, plus stock in the Sawtel companies valued at $128,000 and his Boynton Beach home, valued at $130,000, and his Porsche and Cadillac, valued at around $40,000.

A will filed in 1981 in Palm Beach left the lion's share of the estate to Wilder's parents, while stock in the two companies was left to former business associate L. K. Kimbrell and a couple of racing buddies, Mark Johnson and Charles McDowel.

Almost $200,000 worth of property in Loxahatchee, Boynton Beach, and Fort Lauderdale was left to Vicki Darling, a woman with whom he had had an eight-year business relationship. Darling and Wilder were corporate officers in Wild Palm Kennels, Inc.

Except for Darling, who took Wilder's three English setters and moved north, it will be years before heirs will receive anything from Wilder's estate. And then it will probably be a fraction of the estimated value.

The IRS filed a $345,000 claim against the estate, charging Wilder had failed to pay income taxes in 1980. His estate also owed nearly the same amount— $172,000—in penalties and interest.

The families of Wilder's victims also filed eight separate lawsuits against the estate that totaled nearly $35 million.

Joining the litigants was former business partner L. K. Kimbrell, who sought $165,000.

"When he came back from Tallahassee in mid-March, I asked him if he knew anything about Beth Kenyon or Rosario Gonzalez," Kimbrell said. "I told him if he knew anything he should tell me. He swore he didn't know anything and that the cops were going to blame it on him anyway."

Kimbrell trusted Wilder until Wilder split with his Visa and Texaco credit cards. Convinced Wilder was mad, Kimbrell joined forces with the FBI, not reporting his credit cards missing so they could be traced, and allowing the FBI to tap his phones.

Kimbrell saw his former friend as "running at random, like a runaway freight train. Anything that got in his way, he flattened."

"I wanted him caught as much as the parents did. I have a daughter and a son. I gave the feds as much help as I could."

Kimbrell paid a heavy price for his association with Wilder. Once newspapers linked the Boynton Beach playboy to the kidnappings of Beth Kenyon and Rosario Gonzalez, the bank where Kimbrell did business closed Sawtel's checking account, causing a hundred payroll checks to bounce. After a call from Kimbrell's attorneys, the account was reopened, but Kimbrell found himself making continual explanations to his creditors.

"I had to reassure suppliers that if I'm going to go

out of business, I'm going kicking and scratching and clawing all the way to the ground.''

Sawtel Electric lost a $250,000 contract, and two of the seventy employees quit, unwilling to be associated with the business any longer. Kimbrell changed the name of the company to put distance between himself and his partner's notoriety.

''It was a dark cloud, a stigma,'' Kimbrell said. ''People thought they were doing business with Sawtel, and this guy is out doing what he is doing. I don't blame them. Even though I suppose he deserved to die, it makes me sick that he's dead because we'll never know where the bodies are. My heart goes out to the parents.''

New Hampshire State Trooper Chuck Jellison spent two weeks in the Upper Connecticut Valley Hospital, recovering from the bullet wound that came within an inch of killing him. After his release and an extended paid medical leave, he plans to resume his duties.

On April 20, 1984, the officials in Miami Beach, Florida, announced they planned a hero's welcome for the two men who put an end to South Florida's most infamous criminal.

''We in Miami Beach and the entire nation want to show our gratitude to these two valiant officers who risked their own lives to apprehend Christopher Wilder, the number one criminal who had created tremendous pain through the entire nation and our community,'' Miami Beach Vice Mayor Alex Daoud told a press conference. "We want to welcome them to the city and show our gratitude for courage at its finest hour."

The troopers and their wives were to be treated to a fun-filled, free vacation that included keys to the city, free flights, hotel rooms, and a cruise.

They would be flown to Miami on Eastern Airlines, where a limo would whisk them to their rooms at the posh Fontainebleau-Hilton hotel. They would dine courtesy of the hotel and take a sightseeing trip in their own car, courtesy of Budget Rent-A-Car. They would also be treated to a three-day cruise aboard the Norwegian Caribbean Lines and meet with local dignitaries at a banquet in their honor, when they would receive the city's keys and a proclamation.

The troopers were a little embarrassed by the proposal and reluctant to accept the free offers.

"They are good troopers, and they feel what they did was something any other trooper would have done under the circumstances," said their boss, Major John Richard Campbell.

The two, however, did attend a ceremony in their honor at the statehouse in Concord, New Hampshire, where they received an armful of framed awards and commendations from Governor John Sununu, the FBI, and the State Police.

Among the plaques and ribbons they received was the Medal of Valor, the highest award granted by the State Police.

"It is a very humbling feeling to come here and accept awards for what we are paid to do," Jellison said.

* * *

Colebrook, New Hampshire, settled back to normal, although it wasn't easy. Celebrity dies hard.

Within hours of Wilder's death, one hundred news persons and camera crews were on their way to the isolated logging town. By Saturday, as the *Sentinel* noted, there were so many newspeople that "anyone walking down Main Street or even remotely near the scene who looked the least bit like a resident, was virtually sure to be hailed and asked an interview."

Some welcomed the outsiders. Motels that had to wait until deer season to be full were sold out, even at two and three times the normal rates. And Howard's and Speedy Chef, the only two restaurants in town, did turn-away business through the weekend.

Limousine service also did a brisk business, taking newsmen to and from the airstrips in Bloomsfield and Berlin.

"We would haul them up to the hospital and down to the airport and back to the filling station where they could pretty much walk back and forth to get what they wanted," said Paul of the Peter and Paul Nugent limousine service.

For local news reporters, it was a time to make money and earn national recognition. *Sentinel* photographer Terry Rosi was the first photographer on the scene, and was soon swamped with offers for pictures by major newspapers and wire services. Rosi turned down a hefty five-figure offer from press lord Rupert Murdoch to sell photos to the Associated Press. Backup photographer Ward Thompson, a sixteen-year-old high school student, received similar offers and sold prints to United Press International, *People* magazine, and the *Miami Herald*.

Cameron Howard, owner of Howard's restaurant, was not to be outdone and sold his home video of the shootout to ABC for $2,000 plus royalties. He used the money to take a trip to the Caribbean.

As Colebrook said farewell to the media, the small town of Penn Yan, New York, readied to say good-bye to Dawnette Sue Wilt, the spunky sixteen-year-old who had been stabbed and left to die, but lived to turn the tables on Christopher Wilder.

It was her description of Wilder and the car he was driving that alerted the FBI that he was headed toward the Canadian border.

"The main credit for Wilder's demise lies with Dawnette," said Yates County Sheriff Jan S. Scoffield.

The 6,500 residents of this farming community in the Finger Lakes area felt sympathy for the young girl and her parents. The merchants got together and donated gifts. Restaurants gave gift certificates, the stores gave cosmetics and a radio. Other people sent get-well cards and small gift-wrapped presents. A local company also lent her the use of a private jet to take her parents back to Dyer, Indiana.

Along with the goodness came crass offers of money, as the news media sought interviews and pictures. One tabloid offered up to $25,000 for the exclusive rights to her story.

The family, wanting to protect their badly wounded and traumatized daughter, refused to give interviews or negotiate book and movie rights. Their single public announcement was made on Sunday, April 22, when they read a prepared statement thanking the people of Penn Yan for the kindness they had shown their daughter.

Dawnette did not appear at the press conference, but before she left on the plane home, she left behind a handwritten note of appreciation.

"I would like to personally thank everyone who was personally involved in my recovery," she wrote. "I would like to thank the nurses at the hospital who aren't only women in white, but were my temporary mothers. I also want to thank the doctors who were my eyes and smiles. Because of them I knew my recovery would be fast and complete. Without the strength and love of these people, I wouldn't be leaving within a week's time. They made me feel and see the good in people again. May they always feel my love for them."

Across the country in Torrance, California, Tina Marie Risico went into seclusion while the media haggled over the value of her story.

"There is no question in my mind her story would sell for a million dollars," said Redondo Beach attorney Laurie Belger, who had been retained by Tina's father. "Over the weekend, I got calls from all over the world—Australia, you name it."

Everyone wanted a piece of the survivor. A movie company out of Miami wanted to buy the film rights. A book publisher said he would pay $100,000. The *National Enquirer* said it would top any offer.

Tina's dad said he retained the attorney so his

daughter wouldn't have to face the ordeal of a bloodthirsty, thrill-seeking press.

"I didn't want her put through a press conference," he said. "I didn't want her to face the third degree by fifty reporters with cameras. She has been through enough for nine days."

He said it would be more comforting for her to sit down with one reporter and relate just one time the story of the coast-to-coast journey she made with her kidnapper."

A story, naturally, that went with a price tag.

"I suggested the interview might be sold and the money put in a trust fund," said Laurie Belger. "It could be used for a college education or future psychiatric care."

Dr. Ronald Summit, the UCLA Medical Center psychiatrist, worried about the fragile health of his patient.

"I would think this kind of celebrity status, as a rape victim and as a survivor—the one uncut survivor out of maybe a dozen—can only bring pain to her. And it may draw out a whole army of people who want to test her exploitability. But, then, if Johnny Carson wants her on the show tomorrow night, my advice isn't going to hold a lot of water.

"Ironically, the hope to be recognized as something special, the hope to be able to participate in the glamorous world of modeling led her to trust Wilder in the first place. It is this same need for attention that prompted her to follow Wilder that might place her squarely in the public eye.

"God knows, almost anybody who has any reason

to stand out in the crowd is led to exploit that. That's no less true for Michael Jackson than it is for Tina Risico. This society works very hard to reward its celebrities. Any young person is likely to be drawn into that. I hope that she is not being exploited in it by the advice of adults who want to capitalize on it.''

On Thursday afternoon, May 3, a family was driving west to Las Vegas when they pulled off Utah's Highway 89 for a rest. The heat was intense along the barren, peaceful stretch of desert, and the family wanted to soak a bit of the beauty in before traveling on.

As they parked in a small rest area to swig their sodas, the father strayed a few feet from the car to check out a rock formation. He went about fifty yards before he found Sheryl Bonaventura. The nude body of the blonde lay beneath a gnarled fourteen-foot cedar tree, no more than a hundred feet from where a search party led by her father, Jim Bonaventura, had looked for her.

That evening FBI agent Terry Knowles told the Bonaventuras that the thirty-six-day search for their daughter had finally come to an end.

The pretty blonde who had been hours away from a ski vacation in Aspen with her boyfriend had died like the others, violently and alone. The cause of death was multiple stab wounds, including one that penetrated her heart. She had also been shot once through the chest. The FBI figured that she had probably died on March 31, when Wilder passed through the sandy hill area to get to Page, Arizona.

The tragic news was received stoically by her father, who had joined searches in the mountains and deserts for her.

"If they hadn't found her, we would have had to continue searching. There would always have been hope that she was alive. If you didn't find out, it would eat on you forever. But at least we have our answer."

Sandy Bonaventura says, "These girls did not have to die. Judges, for whatever reasons, let this man go. This man should have been put away years ago. I think the average American citizen had to realize that he or she does not have the rights the criminal does. Where are all these girls' rights? Their families'? If judges don't want to prosecute our criminals, then we need to elect new judges.

"It is not just us that this happened to. It happens to victim after victim. These men are useless to our society, mad demon-possessed men like Christopher Wilder. Let's get rid of him and the other serial murderers who prey upon women. They should never be unleashed on the American public."

Christopher Wilder's criminal case history was once kept in the office of Kim Lalonde, a probation officer with West Palm Beach County. Lalonde recalled her client as not being "much different from a lot of other fellows I see every day. In fact, he was probably better. He cooperated fully and was never late to any of his probation hearings each month. I know he was also keeping his appointments with his sex therapist every two weeks, and that he was supposed to be making progress.''

If there was a problem, it was not in letting Wilder slip through the cracks, but perhaps in the probation system itself.

''Men convicted of far more serious offenses than Wilder are routinely sentenced to probation,'' Lalonde said. ''The way I see it, probation sometimes is just another system to take the financial pressure off the prison system. And probation, coupled with therapy, sometimes works well. But it is hard to tell if therapy will work without some kind of inpatient screening. That takes a lot of money, and society doesn't seem willing to spend it. It's frustrating that no one was able to see just how sick Wilder was and be able to help him before he cracked, but as I said, he wasn't much different from a lot of fellows I see. And I'm not so sure that there isn't someone else out there just like him right now. And nobody has any idea who he is.''

In mid-April the body of a young woman was found in the Ocala Florida National Forest about forty miles west of Daytona Beach. Daytona Beach police first believed the partially clothed corpse was fifteen-year-old Colleen Orsborn, who disappeared from her Daytona Beach home on March 15.

''At this point, I can't say whether it's her or not,'' said Detective Larry Lewis. ''But it looks possible.''

But later a chart comparison ruled out the possibility that the girl in the swamps was Colleen. The corpse has still not been identified, and the search for the missing teen continues.

On June 15 the two-month-long search for seventeen-year-old Michelle Korfman ended when an unclaimed body in the Los Angeles County Morgue was identified through dental charts as the missing Boulder City, Nevada, teenager.

She was discovered on May 11 by two bicyclists who had stopped at a rest area off the Angeles Crest Highway in Angeles National Forest. The body was too badly decomposed to determine a cause of death and had lain in the morgue for over a month, identified only as "Jane Doe 39."

There is no rest, however, for the families of Rosario Gonzalez and Beth Kenyon. Miami police detectives follow up on the occasional tip that is phoned in. But leads are few and far between.

On Mother's Day, May 13, Rosario's parents and two other relatives were arrested for trespassing on Wilder's property in Boynton Beach. They had gone to his home to search for clues that might tell them what Wilder had done with their daughter.

"I told my husband it was Mother's Day and I wanted him to go with me," Rosario's mother said. "We went to the yard and around the pool, looking under trees, in a canal. We knew it was private property, but we thought we could find something that belonged to her. We were just walking around, looking to see if there was any place where land was removed.''

The family was scheduled to appear in court June 14, but the charges were dropped.

''I can understand the mother,'' said Boynton Beach police Captain Carl Dixon. ''She wanted to find her daughter, and it was Mother's Day. She just went about it the wrong way.''

The search also continues for Beth Kenyon. On April 28 a dozen deputies in Colbert County, Alabama, searched in vain for a log cabin envisioned by a psychic as holding the body of the former Orange Bowl Princess. Other psychics have seen the pretty daughter of Bill and Delores Kenyon standing alive in waist-deep water, tied to a tree in a swamp, or dead and buried in a cement coffin.

The Kenyons have searched for their daughter since she was last seen alive on March 5th. They will not rest until they find her—with or without the help of police.

Bill Kenyon says, ''I went along with the police, I was gullible. Now if anybody asked me how to handle a situation like this, I'd say take it into your own hands. Don't count on the police for anything.''

THE SEARCH FOR MISSING GIRLS
By
Judith Knight

["Dozens of psychics and persons claiming psychic experiences have reported 'seeing' Rosario Gonzalez and Beth Kenyon since they disappeared last spring. The two have been 'seen' as far away as Venezuela and as near as suburban Miami. The calls still come in, though not as frequently as they once did, and skeptical police still check them out, when they have something to go on.

[Free-lance writer Judy Knight lives in Delray Beach, just a few miles from Christopher Wilder's home, and has covered his grisly story for *True Detective* magazine.

[Early in June she contacted psychic Judith Field and asked her to use her psychic powers to aid in the search for the two South Florida girls.

[That request led to the following story. "Judith was frighteningly accurate," Judy says. "Tromping through those marshlands with the FBI gave me a shiver up my spine, like a Stephen King Novel."]

I became interested in the Christopher Wilder case just days after he fled Florida. I have friends living in Boynton Beach, and by coincidence I had been visiting a friend who lived just a few doors down from him shortly before he left town. A girlfriend of mine even claims that she met Chris at the Banana Boat bar.

So I was interested in him, if for no other reason than I am a reporter and that I was physically close to one of the biggest news stories of the year.

I also felt compassion for the families of the young women who fell victim to Chris Wilder. For most reporters, the story ended with the bloody shootout in Colebrook, New Hampshire. For those grieving families the story will not be over until all the young girls have been found.

I knew that Miami authorities have been besieged by persons claiming to be psychics. A few were cranks, but most I am sure felt they had seen or experienced something that might aid police.

By nature police are a skeptical breed and they have little use for people with psychic powers. For every prediction that has led to the discovery of physical evidence there have been thousands that did nothing but eat up valuable police time.

So police don't like psychics. They won't always say so, because that might make them appear rigid and close-minded. But they don't like them.

I am a reporter and have written about psychics for years. Personally, I believe that certain people possess certain gifts of sensitivity that cannot be rationally explained. But even if I disbelieved, I would still jump on a psychic story in a minute. People want to know about psychics, and they always make good copy.

It was my reporter's instinct that made me decide to call a psychic I knew to see if she could help find the bodies of Rosario Gonzalez and Beth Kenyon.

Her name is Judith Field, a woman in Ohio whom I knew to have phenomenal mental powers. I'd seen evidence of her startling ability in the past. I had, in fact, written about her for the combined *News of Delray* and the *Boca Raton News* when she'd been in the area for a short time in January.

Currently a minister who is using her remarkable gift to help people, Ms. Field has had successful radio and TV shows in several states. In addition, she is assisting lawmen in the Columbus area without charge.

"I'm investigating the Wilder story," I said to her on an impulse. "Do you see anything on him?"

I wasn't sure she would be willing to concentrate on the question. After all, it was after eleven at night, and "seeing" takes a certain amount of energy. She'd already put in a long, busy day, in addition to caring for a husband and three sons.

"I'm not familiar with it," she said, but agreed to try to pick something up.

An attractive blonde, Judith hadn't been following the reports at all; she was much too involved in trying to solve several tragic murders in the Buckeye State.

She began, however, by describing Wilder just as she did with people who called in to her various ministries on the air. If the description fit, she would continue; if it did not, she would quit, assuming she wasn't making contact—a very rare occurrence for her.

"I'd like to know about the first two women," I told her. "Other psychics have worked on this, and some feel they may be alive." I gave her the names of Beth Kenyon and Rosario Gonzalez.

She wanted to know more about Wilder first—what his full name was. She felt he'd been out of the country, and asked about that. I told her he'd been born in Australia and came here when he was quite young.

"Twenty-three," she interjected. That was close, and I filled her in with the basic details of the case. She continued:

"I get a real funny gut-feeling on the two [women] you just mentioned. I'd be very surprised if they're found alive. I saw one girl with pretty dark hair, real pretty girl—pretty eyes. He usually went with women who had pretty eyes anyway. Now, I saw her face down. I saw fresh block—almost like fresh construction block and I could see the fresh concrete with water around it. She's dead for sure. I saw the other one wedged in somewhere—kinda like when he came at her she was pushed against a wall or something."

I asked her for a location—was the site up this way (Boca Raton, Delray Beach, Boynton Beach)? Maybe, but more west of town there, she said, and probably in construction where wet concrete's been poured over them. Did I know of any commercial buildings— more than one story—that he was working on? I told her I'd check.

"Judy, do you have a place where people eat in the area like 'Soupy's' or 'Snoopy's' or 'Scoopy's' —something like that? Yellow lettering, sells hot dogs—that sort of thing."

I hadn't, but again I said I'd check.

"Did he at any time ever drive a maroon-colored car?" When I said yes, she said, " 'Cause he's had several dead bodies hauled around in that thing. There's something wrong with the brain there. I almost felt like there's a scar on the brain."

Trying further to pinpoint the location of the miss- ing women—possibly some other victim than the two mentioned, Judith said, "He definitely was working a project where there were large banners used, like in colors, like a blue—could be a canopy or something— like a white bird on them, and I felt one girl was under some new floorboards. Dead, though. He was walking back out from leaving her there—a very thin girl. I'd take her for naturally curly, maybe a perm look; maybe more to the red look, but don't forget, if she was dropped she'd have mud on her hair. He usually went for girls with dark hair with those big eyes; that's what threw me on her a little bit."

When I mentioned that he hadn't done away with all the women he knew—that some he was quite protective of—Judith said he "probably had more than one personality."

"I almost felt, like when he was a child back in Australia, that he had witnessed a couple of murders— been part of that as a child. When I saw that, he was probably nine to twelve. He was small for his age, actually. He either witnessed it, Julie, or was part of it."

At this point, Ms. Field "picked up" that Wilder's father had "worked on boats." She saw also that Wilder had "numerous sexual experiences before the age of nine," (which I later verified during an interview with a woman who knew him very well).

She asked if there was another child younger than he in the family, for she saw him as a "living human being walking around when his mother was pregnant." That I later found was true.

Delving deeper, she mentioned that Wilder may have experimented with "black occult" for a while, and even been fascinated by Hitler. "He seemed to need some kind of power over people—had to dominate them. He could be a yeller too. If he couldn't intimidate them [any other] way. Probably those who survived him, that he cared a lot about, just didn't push the wrong button; the others did. He played with people's minds a lot, especially those close to him."

Judith mentioned that sometimes people didn't know him as the same person—that he seemed to be "in disguise" at times and use other names. She picked up the name "George Huntley," which she believed someone had known him by in a city farther south. "So the man did take on other names."

Recalling how he took cards from modeling agencies and photographers, I told her he did. She said he almost never kept his own emotions with another name; he changed his emotions as he changed his name.

"You probably got you somebody with a real multiple personality. He definitely had multiple personalities, because he could stop and help a kitten and show a lot of love and walk all over and try to find it a home." (This I had heard during interviews with his friends. "He helped the whales." "He loved his three English setters." "He was kind to people who needed him.")

"There seemed to be a certain voice tone that set him off," she continued.

At my request, she described some of the women who knew him well. Then she said, "No female would walk away from him after having anything to do with him at all. He could end relationships and that was fine, but if they wanted to end it, even if he didn't want them, he would not let them do that. He couldn't handle rejection. He'd brood for weeks. He didn't like being alone. Very emotionally immature."

Ms. Field then noted that he'd "been ill when he was young. A high temperature. He picked up some kind of infection that caused a lot of this," she said. She agreed it might be encephalitis. This was all Judith Field saw of Wilder that night.

Because I knew how many times her statements had been true in the past, I wanted to check the locale she'd given me for the missing Miami models as soon as possible. The families were heartbreaking as they advertised, listened to every piece of advice, literally beat the bushes to find the beautiful young women. Frustration must have filled them like the steam of an overheated boiler as each lead turned up false. We couldn't help thinking it would be better to know the worst than not to know at all.

My first step was to look for the "place where people ate" named Snoopy's, or Scoopy's, or Soupy's. Looking in both the yellow and white pages of the phone book, I found nothing. I checked the long-distance operator for such a name in West Palm Beach, Fort Lauderdale, Loxahatchee. Nothing. As a last resort, I got the special operator.

"There's a restaurant named 'Scoops' in Boca Raton. Could that be it?" she asked.

I took the number and called; the name was close enough.

Excitement made me hyper as the waitress on the other end of the line answered each question: "Yes, we sell hot dogs. Yes, we have yellow lettering— yellow is our color. We're located way west—on four forty-one at the end of Glades Road."

The place was on State Road 441—as far west as one can get in Boca Raton! And Glades Road was where Boca West was located—where Chris Wilder had been building houses. Judy had surely pinpointed the area.

The next step was to drive about twelve miles south to Boca and about ten miles west where I found Scoops just as Ms. Field had said. It was in a small, very new mall.

West of 441 at the end of Glades there was only land. There wasn't much in the immediate area either north or south either, but along Glades, heading back toward the ocean, there was a great deal of building going on. New construction had also begun in the small mall near Scoops, but it wasn't yet off the ground.

We drove slowly eastward on Glades. A shallow canal and a great deal of wooded land was on the south side of the highway; a small, new section of houses was on the north directly behind the mall. Then, beyond the houses, in a large field with a small lake, stood one lone house close to the road with colored banners flying. It had a bent-over cardboard sign in front of it which, if one looked hard enough, said $99,000 and gave a name and number which I later called in vain. It appeared to be the model for a subdivision which had run out of money. A main street had been constructed around the lake, but no activity was in evidence. A little farther east was a two-story building which might have been recently finished. In fact, the house itself might have been two story.

Walking around the bare front yard, we found cement bags, a stand with new flooring, wiring, and various construction items. There were blobs of cement in what—if one let one's imagination go wild— could have been graves. We dug a little with sticks, to no avail. We tried the door. It was locked. We left. Because of the time, we had to return to Delray Beach.

Actually there were thousands of places where Wilder could have dropped a body and been close to construction, banners, water (and Scoops) in west

Boca Raton. We could see, driving back, that neither Boynton nor Delray fit the clues the psychic minister had mentioned. Everywhere in west Boca, building was going on.

Involved in other research, I couldn't get back to the area at once, although I reported what Ms. Field had said to Detective Tom Neighbors of the Palm Beach County Sheriff's Office. I also told two of Wilder's close friends who had worked for the company for whom he was doing construction—women Judith had "seen" who had only experienced the "good personality" of the man.

The two women, accompanied by their skeptical bosses, drove the few miles west from their place of employment to again search the area of the model house. Then, next morning, with great excitement, they told me what they'd found. Both women and their bosses felt we should call the FBI.

Electrical cord, duct tape, wire, a shovel, cement bags, a length of what they thought was conduit pipe with matter in it that enticed ants, a girl's white top, and a man's Hawaii surfer T-shirt in Wilder's size. One of the women, a pretty twenty-three-year-old who'd gone with him for months, recognized it as being like one she'd seen him wear. He'd stopped off at Hawaii on his way back from Australia and had purchased it there. So sure was she that it was his, she had brought it back to work with her.

Then to top it off, the men had walked directly behind the house a little distance and came to a canal ("water all around"—he always left his victims by water). There they not only saw what looked like graves, they also discovered a Mountain Dew bottle along the deserted, overgrown canal bank.

As soon as they rejoined the women, they asked what Chris liked to drink—beer? No, the women replied, he drank soft drinks—Mountain Dew was his favorite and he always drank it in a bottle, never a can. It was this, perhaps, more than any of the other discoveries, that made them believe they'd found the spot. Besides, they all believed Wilder had worked on this particular house.

Their search had been made on Friday afternoon. I called the FBI on Monday. Already familiar with Wilder's friends, the agents knew the women and met them and the bosses at their work at 2:30 that afternoon.

A few minutes later—with Detective Neighbors, one of the bosses, and me—the agents began their inspection of the property. First, they checked the items found near the model house. Next, they drove behind the house until they were as close as they could go to the canal. From there we walked a little way, climbed down an embankment, and arrived by the water.

Feelings were tense as the men sought clues, placed the soft drink bottle carefully in a plastic bag, and tramped around the underbrush. What would we find? It was frightening to think about.

There were a couple of grave-sized indentations where something had been dug—the sandy soil was loose. There was a dead odor too. It only hit us occasionally and couldn't be located precisely.

"You wouldn't smell it if a body's been out here

for three months,'' Detective Neighbors stated. ''Although I've sniffed out bodies before.''

Probably a dead animal, but . . .

One of the agents had driven to get a shovel. He returned and began to dig. A large piece of shale rock flipped out, making us double-take, it looked so much like bone.

''I'm not sure why I bothered to get a degree,'' the digger remarked as the sand flew. His light remark tended to relieve the tension. At last he stopped. He had hit roots and solid earth. ''Is this enough?'' he asked. The other agents nodded.

The digging had revealed nothing.

After a while, taking the possible links to the dead suspect with them as evidence, the men left.

I too went home. I hadn't lost faith in Judith's very amazing ability. She'd been helping find criminals since the year she was seven and ''saw'' a car thief burying his loot several blocks away from her home. I was only disappointed in my own interpretation of her vision.

Were the victims in the water where Ms. Field had indicated? Or were we following an impossibility? For the families' and lawmen's sakes, I wished the search had ended with discovery.

I would try to reach Ms. Field another day.

Dr. D. G. Boozer
Clinical Psychologist
3419 Acapulco Drive
Miramar, Florida 33023
(305) 961–5582
By Appointment Only

January 2, 1977

The Hon. Marvin Mounts, Jr.
15th Judicial Circuit Court
Palm Beach County Courthouse
W.P. Beach, Fla. 33401

Re: Christopher B. Wilder
    Case #76-2136

Dear Judge Mounts:

In accordance with your Order dated 12/13/76, I have this day examined the above defendant. The following evaluation is based upon clinical interview and psychological tests administered over a 3 hour period.

199

GENERAL OBSERVATIONS: Mr. Wilder was pleasant and cooperative. He verbalized in a rational, relevant manner but at times his speech was stilted and peculiar. Affect was appropriate to his thoughts and his situation. As an interview informant he was not altogether reliable; he would offer statements and then retract them, and at times he contradicted himself. He followed directions rapidly and readily, and appears to be of average or better intelligence. Overtly he was at ease.

INTERVIEW INFORMATION: He is a 31 year old (DOB 3/13/45) American, born in Sydney, Australia. He was educated in the U.S. and is an High School graduate. He has no military service. His occupation is "construction." He was raised in an intact family consisting of parents, 3 younger brothers, and himself; the others live in Australia. Father was in the American Navy for 25 years and is now retired. There is no history of mental illness, nor of arrests. Prior to this arrest, defendant was once charged with Disorderly Conduct, and fined $25.00, in 1970. Father was the boss and the disciplinarian. Defendant was closer to the mother who was warm, too easy and gave them whatever they wanted.

He denies illnesses, accidents and periods of unconsciousness. He has no somatic complaints; he then states he has had stomach problems, since age 18, from nervousness, but has never consulted a physician. Since age 12 he has bitten his nails so that they bleed.

He denies mood swings but once became depressed

and took a package of valiums to calm down. He denies suicidal ideation like "no jumping off a bridge." Later he states he gets depressed but does not show it.

He has one friend that he considers close, otherwise he does not mingle much; he is "self-centered with" his wife. He has no enemies, he is "not an instigator" but he has a bad temper.

Drug history is that he only drinks beer or Tom Collins at times.

SEX HISTORY IS AS FOLLOWS: At age about 14 he touched girls' bustlines. At age 16 he had intercourse to climax with a female age 15, and continued with her for a while. He then began relations with other females, about his own age, until he married, to a frequency of once a week. At age about 11 to 13 he engaged in voyeurism for about 3 months. For the past six years he has attended "adult picture shows" and wants to masturbate but waits until later and then does so to the memory. He has picked up hitchhikers for sexual purposes and even though he thought they might be an easy mark this has not happened. He engaged a prostitute once. He has had no relations with children under age 16 nor adults over age 31. He began masturbation at age about 17 and uses pictures (Playboy Magazine) or fantasies of female breasts. He adds here that he does not use in general anger or anything like that. He masturbates about twice a week. He has fantasied rape, with masturbation, to climax, for the past couple of years.

His opinions about rape are that it is wrong because it is against the law, it might leave scars on the victims, mentally, for the rest of their lives, and it is unethical.

Concerning current charges he relates the following. He has known the victim by seeing her several times in connection with his work. He did not plan to rape her and he had no thoughts of having sex with her. He offered her a ride in his truck, to her home, and she told him she was looking for a job as secretary. He suggested that she apply to his boss but that she dress seductively. She therefore took off her bra and changed to another blouse, one she carried with her. He suggested she undo her blouse and she screamed and he slapped her. They were in a deserted area. He had her masturbate him, manually and orally, to climax. He then took her home. In the interim he apologized and offered to have her take him to the police and he also threatened that he did not know what he would do if she reported this. The victim told him she had been raped before, and the offender was never caught and she wanted no more trouble, her father was strict and she had bad nerves and was afraid the father would find out. He states he slapped her with his hand and is not aware of any more such as that she claims he slapped her around a lot and has bruises to show.

Concerning knowledge of right and wrong, he relates that in his opinion rape is wrong because it involves force, that it is not ethical, and it is against the law, it also can leave scars for the rest of their lives. He adds that he rationalized that it was not wrong but he realizes he probably has created problems for his particular current victim. He states he is now primarily interested in staying out of jail, but he also says he obviously has a problem and would cooperate with a treatment program. Insight concerning why he committed this alleged offense is nil. He does express that on that day he was feeling down and that it all happened like it was in slow motion and he said to himself that there is no way to stop this unless he puts her in a hole and goes away. He discusses marital difficulties but does not relate this to his charges.

PSYCHOLOGICAL TESTS AND INTERPRETATION: He was administered the Bender Gestalt Visual-Motor Test; the Draw-a-Person, Person, House, Tree (DAP, HTP); the Sentence Completion; and the Rorschach.

These techniques do not suggest brain damage, nor mental retardation. Projectives indicate that in structured-type situations he is orderly in approach to problems and plans ahead to some extent. He does not auto-correct, even on hint. Motivation for improvement may be assumed to be poor. He is self-assertive but not aggressively so.

In free situations and when left to his own resources he is also self-assertive, at times passive and at other times aggressive. His reality ties are virtually non-existent and at best tenuous. He shows defective judgment and weak reality testing but has some hold on reality at present. He is tense, fearful, and apt to experience emotional upheavals which result in complete loss of intellectual controls. At such times he may behave in a manner detrimental to the safety of himself or others. He perceives and behaves either in response to the emotional aspects of a situation or his fantasies. He shows almost no ability to consider the objective factors. His fantasy life is generally above the level of awareness and he recognizes, at an intellectual level, his inward turmoil and feelings of helplessness and inability to control what he considers a basically hostile environment. On the positive side, he is able to see things as others do, i.e. conform, and he shows ability to empathize with others. On the other hand, he is over-alert to possible danger, in the paranoid fashion, and inclined to project on to others his own thoughts and emotions. Special problem areas are those concerning his heterosexual role in this society, and his ability to assume the responsibilities of a dominant, male adult. He has also problems concerning male authority figures, and his ability to identify with that figure. Insight (SC) is poor but he does express that he is angry when "pushed and frustrated" and he is "ashamed of himself" and yet is ambivalent as he also says he likes himself and would not want to be someone else. He recognizes that he does "not love others" and is hostile towards controlling persons.

<u>CONCLUSIONS AND RECOMMENDATIONS</u>: Defendant does not appear to be brain-damaged nor mentally retarded. He does appear to be legally competent, at this time. He is presently sane for purposes of trial. He is also a mentally disordered sex offender as per present Florida Statutes. He experi-

ences episodes of extreme emotional upheaval during which he may not be competent nor sane. In my opinion he is basically psychotic and in need of treatment. When not under stress and when in a structured type situation is able to function in an organized manner and appears integrated in his personality functions. When left to his own resources, and under stress, he disingrates, i.e. regresses. He presents a facade, in interview, that covers his underlying psychotic orientation. At this time, he is not safe except in a structured environment and should be in a resident program, geared to his needs.

D. G. Boozer, Ph.D.

DGB/Encs. 4

EDWARD R. ADELSON, M.D., F.A.P.A.
1665 PALM BEACH LAKES BOULEVARD
SUITE 502
WEST PALM BEACH, FLA 33401
TELEPHONE 684–2525

January 7, 1977

Hon. Marvin Mounts, Jr.
Circuit Judge, Fifteenth Judicial Circuit
Palm Beach County Courthouse
300 North Dixie Highway
West Palm Beach, Florida 33401

Re: State of Fla. vs. Christopher B. Wilder,
　　Defendant, Case #76-2136 CF

Dear Judge Mounts:

I saw the above named defendant in my office on 1/6/77 for psychiatric examination to determine if defendant was (1) sane at the time of the commission of the crime, (2) is presently sane for purposes of trial and (3) if defendant is a mentally disordered sex offender as defined in Fla. Statute 917.13.

PRESENT SITUATION: Defendant is presently out on bond following an alleged offense of Sexual Battery, committed on 10/1/76 against victim, a sixteen year old female. Defendant was arrested 10/4/76. The information offered by him corresponds to data of police report and is as follows: Defendant states that he knew the victim by sight, asked her to help him with his car, alleging it was stuck, volunteers in forthright manner that he seduced victim to enter his car and offered to help her get a job with his boss. En route, he asked her to change her blouse, to look more attractive for the job interview, which she did. She had planned to meet a boyfriend later on and had an extra blouse with her. Defendant states that he was fully aware of what he was doing and was conscious of his motives and actions at the time of the alleged offense. However, he adds, that he can not understand why he did not restrain himself at the time and why he could not control his impulses to act as he did. After driving around for a while, he drove on to a side road off Rte. 441, stopped the car, asked the victim to open her blouse, slapped her face when she said no and after she did open her blouse while crying and out of fear, he fondled her breasts. He then drove back to Rte. 441 and then asked victim to rub his penis through his pants and, after exposing his penis, insisted that she take his penis in her mouth, which she did, and then told her to mastur-bate him, using both hands, which she did until he achieved orgasm. Victim then wiped his penis and he proceeded to drive victim to her boyfriend's house. The total time spent with the victim was approximately 45 to 50 minutes. En route to victim's boyfriend's house, defendant asked victim if she wanted him to go directly to the sheriff's office to report the incident, but she said no. Defendant states he knew he had committed an offense, realized he was "in trouble" and wanted to get it over with. Victim states that she was afraid defendant would harm her if she agreed to go to the sheriff's office.

Defendant states that he was then and is now, deeply remorseful and regretful for his actions and does not attempt to condone his behavior. He also was aware that he could be identified by the victim because of his frequent presence during work in that area.

PAST HISTORY: Defendant was born in Australia, moved to U.S. in infancy while his father was in U.S. Navy and made frequent moves every 2 to 3 years as father was transferred to new posts. Defendant spent some time in Birmingham, Ala., Albuquerque, N.M. and Norfolk, Va. He states that he was always a tense, nervous boy and usually controlled his emotions by suppression, but frequently experienced "a nervous stomach" since age 15 and has been a life long nail biter (confirmed). He made a satisfactory adjustment as he grew up, got along well with peers and authority and was an average student, graduating H.S. He served a 5 year apprenticeship as a carpenter from age 16 and has been working steadily at that trade to the present time. He never served in the Armed Forces and never drank alcohol to excess nor took hard drugs or smoked. He is presently on no medication. Except for a few fractures of extremities at age 18 and an episode of difficulty in breathing about 10 years ago, defendant has been in good health. He never sought or received psychiatric treatment. Defendant was not enlightened about sex matters, began to masturbate at 14 to 15 and had his first heterosexual experience at 16. He has had heterosexual relations with several women and states that his sex life with his girlfriend is unsatisfactory and infrequent because of her lack of responsiveness. He denies any homosexual experiences and alleges that he functions normally in heterosexuality. He was never arrested for, nor committed any prior sex offenses. He was arrested once in 1968 on a disorderly conduct charge—a misdemeanor. There is no history of venereal disease.

FAMILY HISTORY: Mother is Australian-born, age 50, and is well and is a housewife; father is 56, American-born, was a Navy career man and retired in 1961 and returned to Sydney, Australia where he lives with his wife. Defendant states that his parents are compatible and that he has always had a good relationship with them. There are 3 brothers.

MENTAL STATUS: Defendant is a tanned, husky, white male of 31. He is friendly, cooperative, appears sincere and forthright, is spontaneous, oriented X3, coherent, relevant and rational. He appears somewhat tense and anxious and evidences a very slight lisp in his speech. Affect is appropriate, judgment (except for the offense) is good, insight is lacking.

He is of average intelligence, there are no halluci-
nations or delusions and comprehension is good. General knowledge is good for world events. Defendant
understands proverbs, does serial 7's well and there
is no evidence of memory impairment. His interper-
sonal relations are good, though limited in social
contacts, and spends most of his time working as a
carpenter, fixing things around his own home and
assists his girlfriend in breeding dogs. He handles his
emotions by control and suppression and is usually
"even tempered." He thinks of himself as generous
and allows himself to be taken advantage of because
of it. Defendant again reiterates his eagerness for
treatment in view of this offense and wants to understand the basis for his recent behavior, acknowledg-
ing that he must have a "problem."

<u>DISCUSSION AND RECOMMENDATION</u>: De-
fendant does not appear to be a mentally disordered
sex offender. He is not insane and does not have a
mental disorder. He has some underlying tension and
anxiety and admits to having committed an offense of
sexual battery. In my professional opinion, he is not
dangerous to others because of a propensity for sex
offenses and therefore does not satisfy the criteria of
a Mentally Disordered Sex Offender as defined in
Fla. Statute 917.13. However, since defendant volun-
tarily admits to having committed an offense of Sexual Battery, he should be directed to receive structured
and supervised treatment for same. Defendant was
sane at the commission of the alleged offense and is
presently sane for purposes of trial.

Thank you for allowing me to examine this defendant and, if I can be of further assistance in this matter, please let me know.

Sincerely,

Edward R. Adelson, M.D.

Diplomate, Amer. Board of
Psych. & Neurol.

ERA/bra
enc.

Please furnish copies to appropriate parties.

ESPIONAGE FICTION BY WARREN MURPHY AND MOLLY COCHRAN

GRANDMASTER　　　　　　　　(17-101, $4.50)
There are only two true powers in the world. One is goodness. One is evil. And one man knows them both. He knows the uses of pleasure, the secrets of pain. He understands the deadly forces that grip the world in treachery. He moves like a shadow, a promise of danger, from Moscow to Washington — from Havana to Tibet. In a game that may never be over, he is the grandmaster.

THE HAND OF LAZARUS　　　　(17-100, $4.50)
A grim spectre of death looms over the tiny County Kerry village of Ardath. The savage plague of urban violence has begun to weave its insidious way into the peaceful fabric of Irish country life. The IRA's most mysterious, elusive, and bloodthirsty murderer has chosen Ardath as his hunting ground, the site that will rock the world and plunge the beleaguered island nation into irreversible chaos: the brutal assassination of the Pope.

Available wherever paperbacks are sold, or order direct from the Publisher. Send cover price plus 50¢ per copy for mailing and handling to Pinnacle Books, Dept.17-345, 475 Park Avenue South, New York, N.Y. 10016. Residents of New York, New Jersey and Pennsylvania must include sales tax. DO NOT SEND CASH.

ED MCBAIN'S MYSTERIES

JACK AND THE BEANSTALK   (17-083, $3.95)
Jack's dead, stabbed fourteen times. And thirty-six thousand's missing in cash. Matthew's questions are turning up some long-buried pasts, a second dead body, and some beautiful suspects. Like Sunny, Jack's sister, a surfer boy's fantasy, a delicious girl with some unsavory secrets.

BEAUTY AND THE BEAST   (17-134, $3.95)
She was spectacular—an unforgettable beauty with exquisite features. On Monday, the same woman appeared in Hope's law office to file a complaint. She had been badly beaten—a mass of purple bruises with one eye swollen completely shut. And she wanted her husband put away before something worse happened. Her body was discovered on Tuesday, bound with wire coat hangers and burned to a crisp. But her husband—big, and monstrously ugly—denies the charge.

ESPIONAGE FICTION BY LEWIS PERDUE

THE LINZ TESTAMENT (17-117, $4.50)

Throughout World War Two the Nazis used awesome power to silence the Catholic Church to the atrocities of Hitler's regime. Now, four decades later, its existence has brought about the most devastating covert war in history—as a secret battle rages for possession of an ancient relic that could shatter the foundations of Western religion: The Shroud of Veronica, irrefutable evidence of a second Messiah. For Derek Steele it is a time of incomprehensible horror, as the ex-cop's relentless search for his missing wife ensnares him in a deadly international web of KGB assassins, Libyan terrorists, and bloodthirsty religious zealots.

THE DA VINCI LEGACY (17-118, $4.50)

A fanatical sect of heretical monks fired by an ancient religious hatred. A page from an ancient manuscript which could tip the balance of world power towards whoever possesses it. And one man, caught in a swirling vortex of death and betrayal, who alone can prevent the enslavement of the world by the unholy alliance of the Select Brothers and the Bremen Legation. The chase is on—and the world faces the horror of The Da Vinci Legacy.

QUEENS GATE RECKONING (17-164, $3.95)

Qaddafi's hit-man is the deadly emissary of a massive and cynical conspiracy with origins far beyond the Libyan desert, in the labyrinthine bowels of the Politburo . . . and the marble chambers of a seditious U.S. Government official. And rushing headlong against this vast consortium of treason is an improbable couple—a wounded CIA operative and defecting Soviet ballerina. Together they hurtle toward the hour of ultimate international reckoning.

Available wherever paperbacks are sold, or order direct from the Publisher. Send cover price plus 50¢ per copy for mailing and handling to Pinnacle Books, Dept.17-345, 475 Park Avenue South, New York, N.Y. 10016. Residents of New York, New Jersey and Pennsylvania must include sales tax. DO NOT SEND CASH.